EDMUND+OCTAVIA

The Dulcie Chambers Museum Mysteries

by Kerry J Charles

An Exhibit of Madness
(Previous Title: Portrait of a Murder)

From the Murky Deep

The Fragile Flower

A Mind Within

Last of the Vintage

AN EXHIBIT OF MADNESS

(Previous title: *Portrait of a Murder*)

A Dulcie Chambers Museum Mystery

Kerry J Charles

EDMUND+OCTAVIA

Cover Image: *Street Scene, Santiago de Cuba*
Winslow Homer, 1885
(Image reversed for stylistic purposes)
This image is in the public domain.

ISBN-10: 0-9963393-1-0
ISBN-13: 978-0-9963393-1-5

Edmund+Octavia, Falmouth, Maine, USA

This book is dedicated
to the one who convinced me
to bring it back.
LYT

CONTENTS

We were created
to look at one another,
weren't we.
— Edgar Degas

CHAPTER 1

Joshua Harriman paused in the foyer of the Maine Museum of Art, holding the outer door open to the cool spring air. The street was quiet, not uncommon for a Sunday evening. He waited until he had completely collected his thoughts. Joshua Harriman was, if nothing else, a deliberate man.

Through the inner door he could hear the music of a swing band, the lively conversations of partygoers, and the pop of a champagne cork. He smiled. Ready. He straightened his silk bow tie and swept through the inner door.

A tray of bubbling glasses greeted him. Accepting one appreciatively, he sipped it while sliding off his overcoat and handing it to the waiter. He scanned the noisy room. The opening was indeed a success. Dulcie had done a perfect job.

Silver rays from the moon that had flickered across the ocean now filtered through the skylights into the cavernous great hall filled with people. The paintings lining the soft gray walls were bathed by gentle spotlights casting a golden glow. The room seemed to shimmer and move with both silver and gold light vying for the honor of most ethereal. The artwork on the walls and Dr. Dulcinea Chambers were the only still, serene elements.

Dulcie, did not feel serene at all. She only stood still in a futile attempt to keep her mind from reeling. She had worked on several gallery openings, and had attended many more, but this was the first that was solely her responsibility. It was her debut as a chief curator, and she did not take this lightly. Her hand shook as she gulped her champagne. She suppressed a sneeze brought on by the bubbles.

Across the room, Joshua Harriman caught her eye and raised his glass slightly, a subtle toast to her success. She waved and, after several moments of wedging her way between the bodies, joined him.

"Dulcie!" he exclaimed and gave her a kiss on each cheek. "You look lovely, dear. Nervous? No, don't be. The opening is fabulous. A gala in the grand style!" He held up his glass and clinked it against hers.

She breathed a long, low sigh of relief. His compliment seemed genuine. "Thank you, sir," she replied. "I'm glad we've been able to get so many people here. It is early, yet, in the season."

Harriman chuckled. "Yes, but that's exactly why we have so many! They're all eager to come out of hibernation," he explained, then glanced down at his nearly empty glass. "Tell me, did you have any trouble locating this marvelous bubbly? I only offered it as a suggestion, a request of sorts. I know you were so busy with all the other arrangements…."

Dulcie laughed, hoping that it would mask her anxiety. "No, don't worry. I had one of the volunteers track it down. I did nothing but sign the order form." She took another gulp from her own glass. "I must say, it was a very good recommendation!"

"Well, it's the little things that matter," Harriman said while casting his eye around the room once again. After he had satisfied himself that Dulcie had everything under control, his methodical mind had already turned to the next task at hand.

He added, almost as an afterthought, "I've learned over the years that the champagne is the key. It must be good enough so as not to offend, yet not so good that the guests feel we have too *much* money. Mark my word, Dulcie, with this champagne you'll be receiving plenty of contributions tonight!"

"I hope so. We certainly do need them," she replied.

Harriman set his now empty glass on a passing tray with one hand and swiftly lifted off a second with the other. "Is that my brother over there? Pardon me Dulcie, but I must have a word with him. We'll talk again later?"

"Of course," Dulcie said, smiling at him. '*I've been dismissed,*' she thought. It wasn't a rudeness on Joshua

Harriman's part, Dulcie knew that. He had simply moved on to the next task on the list. That's what made Joshua Harriman so successful. He always had a list.

Dulcie was relieved by his departure, however. Under most circumstances, she enjoyed his company. At the moment though, she needed to focus on other matters. Graciously chatting with people that she did not know came at an enormous effort for Dulcie, and this evening would require a great deal of it. She felt exhausted already. "He doesn't realize that the champagne was the simplest part," she whispered.

As Chairman of the board of directors for the museum, as well as the museum's acting director, Joshua Harriman exuded the confidence of a lifetime among beautiful things. Dulcie watched him wind his way through the crowd, easily joining conversations, offering friendly comments that made people laugh. Dulcie had awkwardly wedged her way between people to cross the room; Harriman seemed to swirl through them. Until he reached his brother at last on the other side. He gave the man a mock punch in the arm by way of a greeting, which was returned. "And there the resemblance ends," murmured Dulcie.

She turned her attention back to the festivities, trying to convince herself that everything was perfect. '*Except my hair,*' she thought. As usual she had planned to the final second, while completely neglecting the time she would need to get herself ready. '*Thankfully, the chignon is never out of style,*' she thought smoothing back the few dark strands that had fallen across her cheek.

"So you've pulled it off, Dr. Chambers!" The voice spoken directly into Dulcie's ear from behind made her jump. Champagne now dripped from her fingers although somehow she managed to keep it from running down the front of her dress. She growled and turned in annoyance to her brother, Dan. "Great party!" he exclaimed, grinning.

No one could ever be annoyed with Dan for long. He had the kind of face that always seemed to be smiling even when he wasn't, as though he knew a great joke that he was just about to share with you, if only you would stay with him long enough to listen. Dulcie felt her entire body relax. She hadn't realized how tense she had been.

"Thank you! In spite of the fact that you almost ruined my dress, I'll admit that I really needed to hear that. Of course, I only organized. It's Mr. Harriman's money that actually makes it great."

"Never hurts to be loaded," Dan replied somewhat wistfully.

"That's an understatement," Dulcie countered.

Dan sighed and shook his head. "Is he Old Money or *nouveau riche*?"

Dulcie laughed. It was a good question. "The latter, but you'd never know it from his appearance. He has that tweedy, old-leather, *'I've always owned a tux'* look nailed, don't you think?"

Dan nodded, watching Joshua Harriman talking animatedly with his brother across the room. "Yup. 'Course the silver hair doesn't hurt the whole picture either. Looks like he was born to hold a champagne flute." Dan glanced down at his own glass that he held by the stem in his calloused hand somewhat awkwardly. "Me? I was born to hold a beer bottle."

Dulcie couldn't resist. "Why, Dan, you've moved up in the world! Last I'd heard you only drank from cans!"

"Very funny," Dan muttered. He was still analyzing Joshua Harriman across the room. "So how'd Old Harriman get all his money if he wasn't born to it?"

Dulcie smiled. "The usual. A lot of hard work and a little luck. He told me that he started importing when he was only seventeen. He had won a trip to Italy in the 1960's through an essay contest. While he was there, he saw a carved backgammon set that he loved. He didn't have the money for it at the time, but he did take down the name and address of the person who made them. When he got back home he wrote to them, but they'd only ship him ten at a time, so he saved his money then bought all ten."

"Let me guess what happened next. He sold off the nine that he didn't want at a lovely profit."

"Exactly. And so began the import business. He opened a little shop first in Portland, then in Boston. After that he started catalog sales in the 80's, then internet sales, and it mushroomed from there."

"What a way to finance some great travel!" said Dan.

"Absolutely. He has an eye for things. I suppose that's why he's into art as well. He just has a sixth sense for anything beautiful, interesting, and usually expensive. I'm glad I bumped into him when I went to Italy last year. Funny to think I would probably never have this job right now if I'd flown there instead of sailed across the Atlantic."

"That's true," said Dan. "A twist of fate, and all because you don't like to fly."

"I knew it would work to my advantage someday!" Dulcie laughed. "Maybe Mr. Harriman's luck is rubbing off on me. Karma and all that, you know?"

Dan snorted. "Way to metaphysical for me, Dulcie," he replied. "I think you make your luck. It's called *'positioning yourself for the best advantage.'* Think about it. Where were you going in the first place? Italy. You have a lot better chance of bumping into an art-loving multi-gazillionaire going there than going to, oh let's say Siberia, for example."

"But if I had flown on a plane instead of taking the ship, I mean…" Dulcie began to argue.

"If you'd flown first-class you could have just as easily bumped into someone like him," her brother countered.

"Dan, I can't afford fist class. So I think my original point stands." They looked at each other through narrowed eyes. Then they both laughed. Friendly contention had been their mode of communication for years.

Dulcie changed the subject. "What do you think of the new exhibit?" She asked, gesturing around them.

"The what?" Dan asked with a furrowed brow.

She rolled her eyes. "You haven't even glanced at it, have you. Really, Dan, look around. Isn't it fantastic? We've managed to get a work of Winslow Homer's from every one of his major locations except Cuba. We have Paris, Quebec, the Adirondacks, of course Maine…"

"Yes, Dulcie, I read the invitation."

"Really? You surprise me! All right, fine. I won't bore you."

"You do have me intrigued now though, I admit, so I'll ask. What happened to Cuba?"

Dulcie smiled. "Well, hopefully that's the ace up our sleeve. There's one up for auction next Friday at Christie's in New York. It's just a small watercolor sketch, but it would be the final piece for the exhibit. Don't tell anyone yet, but I'm going to make an announcement later tonight that the museum will be bidding on it, and then request donations. I'm hoping to see a lot of checkbooks. You'd better have brought yours!"

"You, dear sister, are ruthless," Dan interjected.

"Hey, it's a tough business. You gotta do what you gotta do," Dulcie concluded.

"True enough. And right now what I 'gotta do' as go introduce myself to that stunning blonde over there," Dan replied. "Who is that?"

Dulcie turned and looked in the direction where her brother's eyes were now glued. The woman that he watched had blonde hair upswept in a French twist, catlike green eyes, and a body-skimming dress that shimmered in silver. "Oh, her," Dulcie said flatly.

Dan laughed. "That good, huh? Guess she has a stunning personality to match?"

Dulcie frowned. "You could say that. She's our benefactor's niece, Alicia Harriman. Her father is Joshua Harriman's older brother." Dulcie nodded toward the two man still chatting across the room.

"She looks more like her uncle than her father," Dan said, unfastening his eyes from Alicia for long enough to glance over at the two Harriman brothers.

"Yes, but don't let that fool you. She does not have Uncle Joshua's good nature. Alicia Harriman is very pleased with Alicia Harriman. Period. You'll get nowhere with her."

"Says who?" Dan demanded.

"Says me," Dulcie quipped. "Your business may be doing well, Dan, but Alicia wants a lot more money than you could offer her."

"Who says I'll offer her money?" Dan asked slyly, wiggling his eyebrows.

"You're pathetic. Go ahead and introduce yourself. I'll watch. You'll fall flat on your face," Dulcie snickered.

"Fine!" he declared. Dan grinned at his sister, then sidled off in the opposite direction from Alicia Harriman, toward the hors d'oeuvre table.

Dulcie scrutinized Alicia. "I can't believe I'm stuck with her for three more months," she murmured. She glanced down at her own dress. It was her standard 'curator black' as she called it, a simple sleeveless sheath in shantung silk, paired with plain black pumps. Her gold chain and diamond stud earrings were the only sparkle in an otherwise traditional outfit. *'I guess I am traditional, more or less,'* she thought. *'I don't want to be the center of attention. This night is about the exhibit, not about Dulcie Chambers. Or Alicia Harriman, for that matter.'* Dulcie unconsciously smoothed the silk over her petite frame and stood up straighter.

Dulcie knew that Alicia would be a handful during the months to come, and, unfortunately in this case, she had Joshua Harriman to thank for that as well. The man could recommend a good champagne, but his choice of employees left a bit to be desired. *'Although I suppose he has little control over who his relations turn out to be,'* Dulcie thought.

Alicia Harriman had begun working at the museum in February as part of a new internship program suggested by her uncle. He had donated an endowment that would fund six-month internships for two graduate students studying art history each year. The choice would be up to Dulcie and a committee of museum officials as to the students selected, except for this first term. Mr. Harriman had requested that he be allowed to choose the recipients of the first two scholarships. Since it was his money, no one could refuse him. Harriman chose his niece, Alicia, as well as a young man named Tom Cole. After meeting Alicia, however, Dulcie wished that she had been allowed a bit more input.

Tom was another matter. She glanced around the room looking for him and saw him at the hors d'oeuvre table talking with her brother. Tom looked as he had in her first meeting with him: a bit rumpled. Dulcie had learned that he was from a hard-working family of lobstermen, the youngest of three brothers. The others had never even graduated from high school, instead dropping out to help with their father's lobstering business. Tom, however, was different. In his interview he told Dulcie that his mother had cleaned houses to send him to college, because he "had a wicked head for learnin'," as she had put it. He was quiet, yet had a biting, dry wit. *'Quintessential Yankee,'* thought Dulcie.

Dulcie had asked Mr. Harriman why he had chosen Tom. Harriman explained that he had met Tom while he was working at the local yacht club where Harriman moored his sailboat. Tom was a launch driver there and, while ferrying Mr. Harriman back and forth to his boat during the summer, had unwittingly impressed Harriman with an unusually large knowledge of art. "He's just the sort of person that deserves this kind of big break to jump-start his career," Harriman had said. "It could be a life-changer for him." Dulcie had agreed.

Both interns had been assigned to work on the Homer exhibit, and Dulcie had to admit each had shown talent although Tom certainly worked harder than Alicia. The exhibit had opened on schedule during the second week of May. Dulcie was very keen on having it open before Memorial Day, the traditional beginning of summer in Maine, and before the auction at Christie's.

The pop of another champagne cork brought Dulcie's attention back to the party in front of her. She glanced at her tiny gold watch and realized that it was time to make the announcement. She took two deep breaths and wound her way through the crowd toward the band. Dulcie nodded at the conductor who nodded back with a smile, finishing the last measures of music with titan blasts from the saxophones. The audience applauded. He turned with a small bow and stepped up to the microphone. "Thank you all! You are too kind. And now, ladies and gentlemen, allow me to introduce the Chief Curator of this fine establishment, Dr. Dulcinea Chambers."

A smattering of applause rippled through the room. Dulcie smiled although she wasn't sure if they were clapping for her or the band. She held the microphone stand with both hands nervously and said, "Thank you all for coming tonight. I didn't expect such a large turnout! I'm very glad that you all love to admire the work of Winslow Homer as much as I do." The audience chuckled. Everyone knew that it was the party that lured them to the museum, not necessarily the art. Dulcie continued. "I would like to first thank Mr. Joshua Harriman for making this evening possible with his superb direction and generous donations," she paused as more subtle applause passed through the audience. Joshua Harriman gave a slight, self-deprecating bow.

Dulcie took a deep breath. "And now, I would like to make an announcement. Speaking of donations," she paused again and the audience groaned. "Yes, you knew an appeal would happen!"

"Nothing like a captive audience!" someone called out from the back. Everyone laughed.

"Almost literally!" Dulcie responded. "But, we do have an excellent cause. Tonight you see on the walls surrounding you at least one work of Winslow Homer's from each of his major locations, except one: Cuba. Next week in New York, Christie's will be auctioning a watercolor of Homer's done in that country. This would complete our collection geographically, and I believe would enable us to draw record breaking crowds to our wonderful museum." The audience chuckled.

"I need your help, however," Dulcie continued. "We do not have quite enough funds in our budget to bid on this work, so I am asking all of you, if you could, to please get out your checkbooks and help us as much as you can. Anything at all is appreciated. Thank you so much, and enjoy the evening!"

She stepped away from the microphone, and the band began to play again. Immediately, three people approached and handed her checks. She thanked everyone graciously and carefully put each check in a zippered leather pouch, worried that she might drop even one. People continued to give her donations as she circulated around the room. Within ten minutes Dulcie realized that she was grinning uncontrollably.

At last the evening wound to a close. Most of the guests had drifted away, and Dulcie retreated to her office to make an initial tally of the donations. She heard the band noisily packing their instruments in the main gallery and looked up as Joshua Harriman walked in holding one last bottle of champagne. "I buried this special one in the bottom of the ice so no one would find it. It's a trick I learned years ago." He showed her the label: Dom Pérignon. "Not bad, eh? Do we have cause for celebration?"

Dulcie pressed a button on her old, battered calculator and said, "Why yes! Indeed we do. Pop that cork and let's toast to our loyal donors!"

Dan stuck his head around the doorframe. "I heard that and, having actually made a donation this evening, I have my own glass right here!" He held it straight out in front of him and followed it into the room. Mr. Harriman laughed and filled it, along with his own and Dulcie's.

Dan turned to Mr. Harriman. With mock sincerity he said, "I don't believe we've met, sir. Dan Chambers is the name. Brother to the famous Dr. Dulcinea Chambers."

Joshua Harriman smiled and shook Dan's hand. "Very good to meet you. I know you by repute, of course."

Dulcie smirked in response as Dan glanced at her with suspicion. She simply smiled innocently at him. "Shall we toast to our donors?" she asked.

"To our loyal donors!" Joshua Harriman replied, raising his glass.

"Hear, hear!" said Dan.

"Well, now! What's this?" A voice dripping with saccharine oozed into the room, followed by a sleek body slinking through the doorway. Dulcie felt instantly cloddish.

"Dear niece, we were toasting our spoils! The museum has done well tonight. Come join us!" Mr. Harriman said.

Alicia smiled at him and batted her eyes at Dan. She nodded once toward Dulcie without even looking at her. "Congratulations!" Alicia said in a breathy voice.

"Thank you," Dulcie answered, wondering if anyone else noticed how phony Alicia sounded. Unfortunately, both men looked charmed. Hiding her annoyance, Dulcie turned to Mr. Harriman. "We really do have a good chance at the painting now, I think. I'll have a better idea as the week progresses. I'm sure more checks will come in, so I'll keep you posted."

"Great!" he said. "Well, this is enough excitement for an old man. I'd best be heading home. Dulcie, thank you for a lovely evening." He raised his glass to her one last time, drained it, then put it on her desk. "Alicia, would you like a ride home?"

"That would be lovely. Good night Dulcie, Dan," she said winking at Dan but without even a glance at Dulcie. Alicia took her uncle's arm and sauntered out of the room.

"Well, Dan," said Dulcie, "at least she knows your name!"

"Yeah, yeah," he sighed. "How about you? Do you need an escort home?"

"That would be very nice, but I need to see everyone else out of here and lock up this wad of cash. Can you wait a few minutes?"

Dan pulled up a chair, sat back, and put his feet on Dulcie's desk. Then he picked up the bottle of Dom Pérignon and refilled his glass. "Be happy to!" he said with a grin.

*I had only to open my
bedroom window, and
blue air, love, and flowers
entered with her.*
— Marc Chagall

CHAPTER 2

Detective Nicholas Black sat hunched at his desk surrounded by the busy sounds of the police station. Computers were clicking, telephone conversations were being held simultaneously on either side of him, and someone in the next room was complaining loudly about the quality of the station's coffee. The detective was oblivious to all of this. He stared at the report in front of him.

"Getting a lot outta that?"

The voice jarred him from his meditations. "Yeah," he replied without looking up.

"Cause you haven't turned a page in ten minutes. Were you in remedial reading when you were a kid?"

Nick picked up his head, looked squarely at his partner, Adam Johnson, and said, "As a matter of fact, I was not. Do you have a problem?"

"Nope. No problem. You just seem a little distracted today. Got something on your mind?"

Nick sighed and closed the report. It was useless to contradict him unless Nick wanted to be goaded for the rest of the afternoon. "All right. Yes, I do." He stopped, and his eyes wandered off into a distant corner of the office.

"Care to share it with me?" quipped his partner.

Nick focused again on the man sitting opposite him. IT was a delicate and potentially embarrassing subject. Nick had worked with Johnson for quite some time now, but he had never been comfortable sharing details of his personal life. Not that he had much of a personal life. Yet.

"All right. You win. Yes, something is on my mind," he replied, taking a deep breath. "Here it is," he muttered while looking around him. He lowered his voice even further until it was nearly a whisper. "I went to that…"

"WHAT?" said Johnson loudly. Three people stopped their conversation and looked over.

Nicholas Black glared at him and continued in an even quieter voice, "I went to that art exhibit opening last night, at the museum." He saw Johnson begin with another quip. Nick silenced him by raising his hand. "Don't even start. No, I was not on duty. And don't ask how I got the invitation - you don't want to know."

"Didn't say I did," said Johnson, trying to hide his amusement. "But if it has anything to do with Betty the

Blonde up at the reception desk, I bet it's a good story!"

Nick exhaled forcefully. It did actually, but he wasn't going to divulge that to Johnson. Nick continued quickly. "Well, while I was at the museum I saw this woman. I wanted to meet her, but couldn't work up the courage to just go and introduce myself."

"Plus, Betty was there and she'd have been ticked off," Johnson guffawed.

Of course that was true also, but Nick wasn't going to fess up there, either. He rolled his eyes at his partner and kept going. "I finally thought of something very profound that I could say to her about the art. It was Winslow Homer by the way, in case you care. So, I walked up to her and casually said something about Homer's ability to," Nick cleared his throat, "*Capture the anger of the sea.*"

Johnson choked back a laugh. "You've got to be kidding!"

Nick shook his head. "It gets worse. She agreed with me, very politely of course, said something intellectual about Winslow Homer, and then excused herself to talk with someone else. At that point I found out who she was. She's the chief curator of the museum. I just stood there holding a glass of excellent champagne with a very dumb look on my face."

"Maybe she didn't think the comment was stupid? If I recall correctly, Homer could paint a mean sea when the mood struck him," said Johnson.

Nick crossed his eyes at his partner. "She's a Ph.D. I'm sure the mood of the sea is more than a little obvious to her. I'm also sure that the thoughts of a moronic police detective are not, shall we say, intellectually stimulating."

"Pardon my mentioning it, but didn't you go to law school? Don't you have a J.D. degree?"

"Well, yes, but I never passed the bar."

"Because you never took it!" Johnson exclaimed.

"All right. You have a point." Nick studied the top of his desk doubtfully.

"And, aren't you, as they say, a man of good taste? Fine wine, is it? I've seen those auction house catalogs in your drawer." Johnson reached over and tapped the top of Nick's desk above the drawer.

Nick glanced over at it. "Well, it's just a hobby. I can't really afford much of it anyway."

"Nonetheless." Johnson eased the large bulk of his body back into the decrepit, gunmetal gray chair and folded his arms. "Should think a smart fella like yourself could come up with an excuse for asking a lady out."

"Maybe," Nick said without much conviction.

"*Maybe* nothing! You've got brains, and you can work a crime scene, not to mention an entire investigation, better than anyone I've seen come through this department. And I've seen quite a few, trust me. You don't have much confidence when it comes to the opposite sex, though."

"Don't have much experience. That's why," Black said quietly.

Johnson grinned. "Oh! Well, if that's the case, then my cousin has this friend...."

"Shut up," said Nick, standing up. "Want to get a real cup of coffee?"

"Yeah, let's get out of here."

The two snaked around the maze of desks and through the large, bulletproof glass lobby doors. Johnson noticed Betty trying to get Nick's attention as they passed by, but decided not to interfere. Best to leave that one alone for the time being. He and Nick crossed the street and continued in the direction of the waterfront toward their local haunt for coffee, simply known as Roasters. It was their second office, due largely to its proximity to the police station, not to mention its superior coffee. Of course, anyone on the force would have agreed that stagnant well-water would be superior.

The coffee shop's plate glass windows overlooked Commercial Street. Right on the edge of the trendy Old Port district with its upscale shops and bars, Roasters also served the island commuters from the nearby ferry terminal and the ship workers at the local dry dock. It was balanced between two worlds, not unlike Nicholas Black, although Nick would have considered himself teetering rather than balanced.

They got their coffee in large paper cups and sat in a booth. Johnson typically preferred the booths to the spindly café tables and chairs. He secretly thought that one might collapse under him, so he avoided them whenever possible. They sat in silence for several moments. Neither touched his coffee yet, knowing from experience that they had to wait at least five minutes for it to cool.

Adam Johnson, a happily married man, felt it was his duty to assist his partner in reaching the same harmonious state, or at least to tease him unmercifully until that time came. Nick was looking like such a lost puppy though, that Johnson decided to go easy on him for the moment. "So, what did you notice first about her?" he asked, finally taking his first sip of coffee.

Nick was reluctant to answer. His dark gray eyes closed for a moment as he thought. "Don't know. I guess her manner. She seemed so quiet and self-assured and intelligent. I should have known she was somebody at that event. It's odd — there was a knockout blonde in a skin-tight dress there too. Every single, and not so single, guy's eye kept straying to her, but she didn't do it for me at all. Too obvious. This other woman, Dulcinea Chambers is her name, was, well, I guess subtle is the word."

"Yeah, and you were so subtle that she doesn't even know you exist."

"Yeah, I hope not after that encounter," Nick shuddered. "Maybe I should think up a reason to meet her… again?"

"Well, don't be thinking too long. Women like that don't stay single forever. Just ask my wife!" Johnson grinned.

The men finished their coffee and walked back out onto the sidewalk. A stiff, chilly breeze had blown in from the bay, although the sun was still bright. Johnson grunted at his partner, gave him a mock salute, and turned back toward the police station. Nick turned in the opposite direction and wandered down Commercial Street, unsure of his destination.

They were between cases. They both hated these lulls. Nick felt anxious when he had little to do and created projects to keep himself occupied. Was this interest in Dulcie Chambers another little project? He wasn't sure. Generally his projects involved multiple trips to the hardware store or the purchase of large, expensive items that depleted his savings. His wine collection began as a little project during a particularly long, cold winter. Now it bordered on obsession.

He thought about Dulcie Chambers again. He had an odd feeling about her, and in his line of work, he had learned to trust his feelings. Strange, though. He knew he was attracted to her, but something else urged him toward her. Perhaps a trip to the art museum was in order?

He turned the corner and walked slowly down the cobblestone street, absentmindedly observing the old brick buildings of the city. He loved Portland. He remembered coming to the city so many times when he'd been a kid. Nick's father, a highly successful Boston attorney, had frequently rented summer houses for his family on different islands in the bay. He remembered taking the ferry boat into Portland once or twice a week, just for fun. The islands, the city, Maine in general had always felt safe to him. As an adult he had learned otherwise, but then again, no place is completely safe. He'd be out of a job if it was.

Nick lived in the city now, a third-floor, walk-up apartment in one of the crumbly brick buildings of the Old Port area. A far cry from the comfort that he had been raised in, it didn't have much of a view, or much floor space for that matter. It was also over a bar, which had kept him awake on more than one occasion. His salary as a detective was certainly not what he would have made as an attorney. *'I can't help it, though,'* he thought. *'It's under my skin now.'*

Nick crossed the street. The Maine Museum of Art was just ahead. He hesitated for a moment when he reached the door, then took a deep breath and went in. The young woman at the reception area greeted him and asked if he was a member. At that moment, Dulcie walked out of her office, smiled at him and pulled out a large binder from behind the desk. She had begun to walk back in to her office when Nick said, "How do I become a member?"

Dulcie turned and smiled again. "That's what we like to hear, Rachel, isn't it?" The young woman at the desk giggled in response as Dulcie disappeared into her office.

"Individual memberships are seventy-five dollars a year," she said. Nick pulled out his wallet. He would have given her twice that for another smile from her boss. He filled out the form she slid in front of him, barely noticing what he was writing. She handed him a brochure, and he began strolling through the main gallery.

The Homer paintings surrounded him. He had not been able to see them very well at the opening, and now he viewed them with interest. Nicholas Black knew little about art, but he knew what he liked. Many of the works were vivid watercolors of fish and animals. The colors were amazing and the wild feeling that emerged from each painting was almost tangible. Life, death, nature's peace and harsh realities were splashed in front of him. Nick drifted silently from one to the next, caught within each frame.

"Those were done in the Adirondacks," a quiet voice said behind him. Jarred from his thoughts, he spun around quickly. He found himself staring at Dulcie Chambers. He was not accustomed to being caught off guard and could not speak. "Homer loved the area. He was a great sportsman," Dulcie continued.

Nick tried to regain his composure. "Yes, that shows in his work," he said.

"If you have any questions, just ask any of the staff," Dulcie said. Then, looking at him more intently, she asked, "Have we met before?"

Nick swallowed hard. "Not exactly. I was at the opening on Sunday. You may have seen me." He hoped that she wouldn't remember his ridiculously obvious comment. "I'm Nicholas Black." He stuck out his right hand awkwardly.

"Dulcie Chambers," she said shaking his hand. "I thought I recognized your face. Did you enjoy the party?"

"Yes, I did. Very much," he answered, trying hopelessly to think of something intelligent to say.

"Good! Well, enjoy the exhibit as well. I'm glad you came back. Most people just go to openings for the champagne and social connections. They don't bother to actually look at the art. Nice meeting you!" She smiled and left the gallery.

"Nice meeting you, too," Nick whispered. He continued to wander through the rooms but saw nothing.

○ℬ

Dulcie walked across the wooden floor of her office and held a print up to the light from the window. The colors were beautiful. Subtle. She squinted at it. It was not a large painting, or one of his most well-known, but anything of Homer's these days would draw a crowd of bidders. She desperately wanted the museum to have it.

Her arm dropped to her side and she gazed out the window. It was a beautiful day in Portland. The sun streamed through the clouds and glistened on the water. In the harbor she watched a passenger boat slowly come into view, and a smile spread across her lips. She put the print on her desk and opened the window.

The boat slid easily alongside the dock, close to the museum building. Its captain, a sandy haired and suntanned man, eased the gangplank into its position. Slightly sunburned passengers, happy after their tourist trip around the bay, slowly made their way to dry land. Dulcie watched as the captain assisted some of the ladies, especially a few of the younger, more attractive ones. She laughed to herself. *Just like Dan, always there to lend a hand. Especially if there's a pretty face involved.* As if he had read her thoughts, the captain looked up toward Dulcie's window. He raised one arm to shade his eyes from the sun, and, spying her, waved vigorously with the other. Dulcie waved back. He pointed to himself, then to the building. Dulcie waved again and stepped back from the window.

Fifteen minutes later, she heard her brother's hearty laugh in the foyer beyond her office. He stepped in, shaking his head. "That Rachel. She's a hoot!" He slid himself easily into a chair by Dulcie's desk.

"Yes, especially when you get her going. Now I have to settle her down if I want to get any more work out of her."

"Don't worry. She's a good girl. Send her on an errand or something."

Dulcie laughed. "So, Dan, how was the cruise this afternoon? Any 'man overboard' drills?"

"Nope. Just the usual stuff. We had a little kid throw up, but beyond that, nothing exciting."

Dulcie made a face. "Yuck. Hope it was over the side!"

"It was. His mother practically dipped him in the water when she saw him turning green. Poor kid."

"But he was all right?"

"Sure. By the time we got back he'd eaten an entire bag of salt'n vinegar chips and an ice cream sandwich. Speaking of food," he paused for a moment, pulling out a thick leather wallet from his back pocket, "I believe I have enough here to treat my sister to a beer and a bowl of chowder. Are you up for it?"

"That would be great! I have more to do here though, for probably another hour or so."

"That's okay, I have to batten the proverbial," he paused, looking out the window, "and not so proverbial, hatches. Meet you at Durwood's? I'll be the one at the bar." He stood up and headed for the door.

"Just don't get too far ahead of me!" Dulcie called after him. She heard his laugh echo again in the foyer.

A breeze from the bay made its way into Durwood's through the door that led to the outside deck. Someone had propped it open with a chair to let in the fresh spring air. Several paper napkins fluttered off tables sending diners lunging for them. A paper plate launched into the air. Everyone laughed when a waiter caught it mid-flight as he stepped through the doorway. He bowed with a grin, accepting the applause.

The waterfront chowder house had just the right balance of paper plates, fried clams, and cold beer. Dulcie surveyed the room and saw her brother sitting at the bar, talking with a ponytailed waitress in cutoff shorts and a snug T-shirt.

"Dulcie!" he gestured for her to join him. "I'm sure this beautiful creature would be happy to bring you a pint of what I'm having!" he said as Dulcie approached. The waitress blushed, giggled, and scurried behind the bar.

Dulcie shook her head. "You are incorrigible!"

"Not at all. I just know how to have a good time, that's all. And, I do believe you envy me for it, sometimes."

She laughed. "You know, sometimes I do!" The waitress slid a glass of ice-cold beer over to Dulcie who nodded her thanks. She sipped it, and then had to wipe the foam from her upper lip.

Dan chuckled at her. "You'll always be a rookie," he said, shaking his head. "However, on a different note, where you're definitely not a rookie, how's the latest project?"

"Going well," she replied, swirling her glass in a futile attempt to clear out the foam. "I've counted up the spoils from Sunday night's soiree and the sum looks quite favorable. Plus more checks rolled in today."

"Can the museum afford it, then?"

"I think we can. I've got to talk with Mr. Harriman in case we need a little extra to put us over the top, though."

"I still can't believe my sister handles a budget of millions."

"Only a budget. The accounting is in far more capable hands."

They were silent for a moment. Dan inspected the amber liquid in his glass, then took a large swallow. Dulcie watched him as he slowly savored the brew. He rolled his eyes to the heavens. She laughed. "It takes so little to please you."

"And that, dear sister, is why I lead a happy life. I have a thriving business, good beer, fine food," he winked at the waitress who had just plunked a basket of fried clams in front of him, "and I live in the greatest place on Earth. The only thing missing is the wife, but I think I'll wait a few more years on that." He was appreciatively watching the shapely waitress walk away.

"Truly, you're incorrigible," Dulcie laughed, accusing him again.

"And proud of it. So how about you? Any winners in the dating game lately?"

Dulcie sighed. "What dating game? I've been so busy lately with the museum, I haven't even had a chance to meet anyone, let alone actually go on a date."

Dan shook his head. "Not good. You need to circulate."

"With whom, I'd like to know."

"Well, what about the opening? Did you meet anyone?"

"Yes, I met everyone."

"…significant?" Dan said, raising his eyebrows.

"Not to my recollection. Dan, I was working. I wasn't thinking about being particularly alluring. Besides, Alicia must have cornered the market there."

Dan smiled. It was not a pleasant smile. "She's alluring, yes, but not in a completely positive way. When she talked with us after the party, in your office, she looked at me like she was sizing up a kill. Made me shudder."

"She makes me shudder on a daily basis, and she annoys me." Dulcie stole one of her brother's fried clams and dunked it in cocktail sauce.

"Why is she interested in art? It doesn't seem to suit her. You'd think she'd be a ruthless executive or that she'd be working over some old rich guy, waiting for him to drop so that she could get his money."

"I agree. I can't quite figure it out either. Maybe she thinks this will help her get more money from rich Uncle Harriman?"

"He looks like he's as fit as a fiddle. She can't hope to get it in his will. That could take years!"

Dulcie sipped her beer. "No, I think she's hoping to ingratiate herself so that he supports her, or at least subsidizes her career. Working in museums isn't exactly lucrative. Alicia is very smart, but I think she's really quite lazy. And selfish. She'll work just hard enough to get what she wants, but no harder."

"Well," Dan said hesitantly, "you could be right. But, I'm no longer interested in her, in case you were wondering."

"I was not," said Dulcie, "Although I think you've made a wise choice. Now where is that waitress? I need some chowder. I think you scared her off, making eyes at her like that."

"Not a chance," grinned Dan.

The children of a fisherman and an island schoolteacher, Dulcie and Dan had the coast in their blood. Dan had planned to continue his father's business and had learned the entire trade while working with him each summer. After finishing high school, Dan continued to fish every day, rarely even taking a break on weekends. The living was difficult. Each year became worse than the one before due to overfishing, pollution in the water, and many, many other problems. Some years they barely made enough money to pay the bills. Dan watched his father's health and spirits decline and knew that these contributed to his early death.

He never discussed these matters with his sister. Only once had he given vent to his true feelings, on the day after their father's funeral. Dan had been very angry and had released his frustration in a stream of disgust for the world and the life that had killed his father. Dulcie had cried bitterly, and Dan never spoke of it again. He could not bear to make his sister unhappy after all that they had been through.

Dan knew then that it was time to move on. If he continued with the family business, his spirits would decline as well. He sold the fishing boat and bought a small passenger ferry, dubbed the Nora May II. His plan was to run harbor tours during the warmer months, as well as to rent it out for parties.

Dan soon discovered that he preferred the company of many people on the boat to the hours of solitude as a fisherman. He happily woke each morning hoping for a clear day so that he could show people his beautiful bay. The early morning tours were always the best. He filled several thermoses with coffee, bought large boxes of donuts, and helped his sleepy passengers climb on board. The bay was often still as the sun rose over it. He pointed out seals swimming by, staring with huge dark eyes at the tourists on the boat above before sliding below the surface of the water. Cormorants stood on rocks, spreading their wings to dry them in the morning sun. On occasion a whale spouted at some point distant from the land. The passengers on these morning cruises were always the most interested in nature. Afternoon passengers were often hot, tired, and simply wanted to sit down and feel a cool ocean breeze. Dan enjoyed both. His business had done well and he was now beginning his fifth year.

He and Dulcie finished their dinner, said goodnight, and parted company. Dan was going to a nearby tavern, as Dulcie knew, to see his latest squeeze, another dark eyed waitress. Dulcie walked slowly back to her townhouse.

'I love Portland,' she thought. *'It truly has its own personality.'* Extending out on a peninsula reaching into the bay, it represented the Yankee way of life in a geographic perspective: connected yet independent. *'That's what I like best about living here,'* she thought. *'People look out for each other, but no one interferes. I feel strong here.'* It was an odd thought: to feel strong simply due to the nature of others. It was difficult for her to explain, but she understood it well. When others do not interfere, you need to be self-sufficient. In a society where you have to ask for help, you learn when help is definitely needed rather than when it is simply a convenience. She inhaled deeply, breathing the strong, sweet smell of the ocean air. That gave her the most strength of all. She turned the final corner to her street.

Stockley Street had a slight curve so that she could not look directly down it to see her house. All of the buildings were brick. In fact, much of the city was brick. Only the more modern buildings were made of concrete or granite or similar gray materials. Dulcie believed, without any foundation, that the warm color of the brick made people happier. At least, it made her feel happier. She walked up the steps to her front door and turned the key in the lock.

Her home was small but beautifully situated. It sat among a row of townhouses on a little hill that overlooked the bay. Her living room faced the bay, while the dining room on the front looked down the curving street. Tossing her purse in a chair by the door, she crossed to the living room. Stopping in the middle of the room, she stretched her arms up over her head and closed her eyes. "A mentally exhausting day," she concluded. "I know I won't get much sleep before Friday. Too much fretting." She dropped her arms, opened her eyes, and went directly to her wine rack. She ran her fingers along the bottles. Pinot? No. The Châteauneuf-du-Pape would do. Uncorking it, she left it to breath while she went into the bedroom to change her clothes. The evening was cool, so she pulled on an old pair of chinos and a cotton sweater. Slipping into espadrilles, she padded back to the wine bottle and poured. It flowed into the glass like a soft purple river. Dulcie swirled it, watching it cling, then inhaled its sweet scent. She tasted it and smiled. '*A good wine and a good man,*' she thought. '*Now all I need is the latter.*'

The light slowly faded over the bay. Dulcie read until it was too dark in the room to see properly.

CHAPTER 3

Alicia Harriman sat in an overstuffed, tufted, black leather chair in her Boston hotel room staring at the ocean perfectly framed between green velvet curtains. Her artfully tinted blonde hair was pulled tightly away from her face into an expensive silver barrette. Her eyes showed traces of wrinkles around the outer edges. Her brow was furrowed.

She was nervous, an unusual feeling for her. She toyed with her glass of gin and tonic, swirling the contents and listening to the ice tinkle. Eleven o'clock in the morning. A little early for a drink, but she had good reason. Her bank accounts and credit cards were unusually tight. She had received two notices and a telephone call within the past week threatening to take action if she did not provide payment. Alicia needed money and she needed it quickly. She took another sip of her drink.

The usual sources had been tapped out. Her assortment of friends, if they could be called that, had given her meager resources for the few favors that she had granted them. Alicia knew that they were beginning to tire of her company. They were on to her game. She needed to start fresh.

The ultimate solution was daunting. Alicia knew that requesting – begging was perhaps the more appropriate term – for assistance from her uncle was nearly out of the question. He had made that very clear in previous conversations. This time, however, she did not know where else to turn. The thought of her belongings being repossessed was not only frightening but also repulsive.

She sighed loudly. This summer was shaping up to be the most boring, frustrating season of her life. She hated living in the tiny city of Portland. She snorted, thinking the word 'city' hardly applied. Internships at the Met and the Whitney in New York as well as another at the National Gallery in Washington had not come through. She had counted on being awarded at least one of them. As an alternative plan she had even applied to the Museum of Fine Arts in Boston, but they had refused her as well. *'Can't these idiots see my talent?'* she thought. Apparently not.

Alicia had grown used to getting whatever she wanted. Her looks and manner more often than not provided the appropriate visa for entry into nearly any venue. If that did not work, her money bought her way. Until recently she'd had an ample trust fund at her disposal. This was how she had ultimately been accepted to the graduate program at Harvard: a private interview with a key, male member of the department, sufficient money to ensure that she could easily cover full tuition, and the name Harriman. She knew that they assumed she would lobby her well-known uncle into making a few generous donations. She even alluded to the possibility, knowing full well that Uncle Joshua only supported smaller charities and institutions.

She would have to qualify herself into one of those categories, however, if she expected to receive any funds from him. Tuition bills were coming soon and she had nothing. Perhaps that was the way to approach Uncle Joshua? He believed in hard work toward a good education. She could simply ask for the money to cover her tuition: a scholarship of sorts. He need not know that a little would be diverted elsewhere. Surely he would not deny her an education!

An even better strategy occurred to her. She reached for the telephone and dialed.

"Daddy?" she said sweetly.

"Yes, Alicia. What is it?"

"I have a really big problem. I just looked at my bank statement and I don't think that I can pay my tuition bill for school! What should I do?"

"Alicia! What happened to the money in your trust fund?"

"Daddy, it's all gone! Harvard is so terribly expensive! Plus, I have to buy books and supplies! And there were the trips for my art studies in Europe. It just adds up, but it really is such a good education, and puts me in the best position to work with one of the major museums." Her voiced dripped like syrup.

"All right, honey. I know. I've just been a little concerned lately about money too. How much do you need?"

"About twenty-five."

"Hundred?"

"Thousand." Alicia heard only silence on the other end of the phone. "Daddy?"

"Yes, I heard you. All right, Alicia. I can't possibly cover that amount, but I'll talk to your Uncle."

"Oh, thank you Daddy! You're the best!"

"Well, we'll see," he mumbled by way of a good-bye.

Alicia put down the receiver, smiled nastily, and tossed back the rest of her drink.

Life had never been terribly difficult for her. This was probably the most trying situation that she had yet faced. True, there had been the trouble with Biology while she was an undergraduate at Wellesley, but thank god for male professors, she thought. She had managed to pull off a B grade. "For my effort, I should have gotten an A," she said to herself, but laughed at the image of the idiot locking his office and sloppily kissing her. *It takes so little to please some people,* she thought. The interlude had been less than pleasant for her, but she walked away with a passing grade. It was all that she needed. She had even stopped attending class after their liaison. It simply wasn't necessary.

This problem was a bit more sticky, yet she was sure that it was nothing that she could not overcome. She stood and began to pour another drink, then thought better of it. "No, I believe I'll go visit the little museum at the Augusta Academy today. Perhaps I can take a look at those new Peales they've unearthed." She picked up the phone.

"Yes, get me the number of the Augusta Academy, please." She waited a moment, then snapped, "Yes, of course I want you to dial it!"

The phone clicked through. "Hello?" Alicia's voice now dripped. "Alicia Harriman here from the Maine Museum of Art. Could I speak with your chief curator, please?" She waited. "Hi. Alicia Harriman here, from the Maine Museum of Art. I'm in Boston today finishing some work on another project, and have the afternoon free. Would it be possible for me to come around and see those new Peales that I've heard so much about?" she waited. "Yes, I hear they're exquisite! …Titian Peale did most of them? How interesting! Would one o'clock be all right? …Perfect. I'll ask for you at the front desk. Thank you!"

She changed out of her fluffy Turkish terry bathrobe and into an oyster gray silk business suit. After all, she was on business, of sorts.

ა

Joshua Harriman sat in his study perusing the mail. The French doors leading to the porch were open and a cool breeze flowed in from the ocean. The sheer white curtains fluttered. He took a deep breath of the fresh sea air. Beyond his study the doorbell rang. He heard his housekeeper, Mrs. Whipple, waddle across the hall, then the sound of his brother's voice drifted toward him. Harriman rolled his eyes. *'What could he possibly want now?'* he thought. Morning calls from Jim were not paid just to chat.

James Harriman came into the room with a hesitant step. "Not interrupting, am I?" he asked Joshua.

"Not at all. Come in, come in." Joshua Harriman motioned toward a heavy antique chair facing his desk. "What can I do for you?"

"Well, I'll get right to the point. It seems that my daughter does not have enough money to cover her next tuition bill. I don't have that amount either. Her mother has been overstepping her bounds a bit recently and I've had to pay a few of her bills, so, anyway, I promised Alicia that I'd speak to you."

Joshua sat back in his chair, clicked the cover onto his fountain pen and tossed it on the desk in front of him. "Jim, you've got to put your foot down with those two women! Alicia doesn't know the meaning of the term 'budget' and as for your EX-wife, didn't she get everything that was coming to her in the divorce settlement?"

"Well, yes, but she keeps hounding me for more, saying it's for Alicia, and I just have trouble…"

"You have trouble saying NO!" Joshua roared. "So I'm going to say it for you! NO! I will not give that spoiled daughter of yours one more nickel! I've already given her a damned good job for several months, which will look very impressive on her resume, and it provides a tidy income as well. Let her get a loan, or even, heaven forbid, take a year off from that snooty school and work for a living like the rest of us!" He stood and paced around the room.

Jim gaped at him. "You won't help?" he finally said. It was more a statement than a question.

Joshua turned to face him. He said very quietly, "No, I will certainly not help. Giving your daughter any more money is not helping. She needs to learn how to earn a living. My greatest fear is that it's now too late for that lesson. I must be firm this time, Jim, and you should be, too."

James Harriman got up from his chair with some difficulty. His head was hanging. "You're right," he said. "I'll tell her to take a year off from school and work. She can live in the townhouse with me and save some money. Thanks anyway, Josh." He shook his brother's hand and crept quietly out of the room.

Joshua shook his head when his brother was gone. Weak. That was the only word that could truly describe Jim. The poor guy was weak in spirit. He never could face up to anyone. Joshua had come to his rescue many times over the years. This time, he knew that someone had to teach Alicia a lesson. Her father wasn't about to do it, and her mother never cared. That left him, although he knew that she would be outraged.

"We all have to get our hands dirty sometimes," he said to no one. As if to demonstrate, he unbuttoned the sleeves of his crisp white cotton shirt and rolled them up. He had a busy day before him.

He turned to his mail, stacked neatly on the desk. Most of his correspondence involved his business and his work with the museum. One letter caught his eye, however. It was addressed by hand in script on a small, pastel blue envelope. "A bit old-fashioned," he murmured with a smile. He slipped the sharp silver letter opener under the flap and ripped it open with one quick motion. It contained a single page. As he scanned it his smile faded. His lips moved while he read through it a second time, as though this would help him to better understand the words before him. When he was through, he groaned softly and let the page fall from his hand onto the desk. He turned in his chair and stared out the window, rubbing his forehead. *'Why bring up the past?'* he thought. *'What's done is done. I didn't know. I'm doing what I should now.'* He scowled as he looked out the window, until Mrs. Whipple tapped on the door.

"Got some nice hot coffee for ya."

"Thank you," he said distractedly, and waved his hand to the corner of the desk.

Mrs. Whipple set down the tray with a clatter. "Gonna be a nice aftah-noon, I think."

He continued to glower out the window. "Perhaps," he said quietly.

Mrs. Whipple looked at him quizzically. It was not like him to be difficult in the mornings. It was not like him to be difficult at all, generally, unless he was pressed for time.

Mrs. Whipple did not make it a practice of listening in on her employer's conversations, but if she was dusting in the next room, well, she might just happen to catch a word or two. She had stepped back into the shadows in time to see James Harriman slink out.

"Big brother thought he could get another handout," she said to herself as she left Mr. Harriman to his brooding in the study. Mrs. Whipple returned to the kitchen and began her own brooding. *'Guess we've all got family problems. And money problems,'* she thought grimly. The subject was never far from her mind, ever since her husband had lost his job the previous year.

Jed Whipple had been spending more time at the racetrack after that. For a brief time during the winter months she had thought that the worst was over. He was staying home more, had actually applied for a few jobs, and did not seem to be stealing funds from their bank account as much. Then she learned about his private little stash: a separate account at a different bank. She had found the statement one night in the pocket of his shirt after he'd fallen asleep in his chair, deep in a drunken stupor. She remembered how the shirt reeked of whiskey and cigar smoke. The chair stank of cigarettes and had small burns on the arms because he so often couldn't be bothered to find an ashtray.

Jane Whipple was beginning to hate the man that she had fallen in love with thirty years before. When she confronted him about the bank account, he had laughed at her. "My money," he had said. "Won it fair and square. Trifecta at the Fryeburg Fair last October." He had been using that to finance his winter bets.

She now fumed aloud, "While I'm here bright and early every day, working hard! Damned fool!" She wasn't quite sure, however, if the fool was him or herself.

The local racetrack closed during the winter, so her husband had found a bookie. His winnings had dwindled to nothing, and now, with the springtime, he was back at the track. '*Picking up where he left off,*' thought Mrs. Whipple. '*Well, he's not gonna get a penny of my money this time. Have to find his own supply. Have to get a job!*'

She opened the shiny stainless steel refrigerator. Smoked salmon. Brie. Champagne. And not that cheap stuff with a plastic cork. This was some French bottle. Mrs. Whipple scrutinized it and felt a wave of envy wash over her. "Not fair," she muttered. It was not fair at all that some people had everything while she had nothing. She worked just as hard, didn't she? Of course she did. She tasted a piece of the salmon. 'Fish,' she said. "Taste's like fish. That's what I grew up on. Grew up on lobstah, too. I see them rich folks pay foh-ty, fifty dollahs for a lobstah dinnah. We got 'em for free and boiled 'em over a bonfire. No damned deli-cah-cy in that! And this salmon. I seen bears on TV eatin' this stuff. No damned fancy stuff here neither!" She closed the refrigerator door with a bang and began to scrub the already sparkling sink vigorously.

Jane Whipple was not truly angry with Joshua Harriman. She was angry with her husband. She was angry with the world. She was angry with herself. The inequities of life seemed to tip toward her side of the balance all too often. Her husband had lost his job. Her husband drank. Her husband gambled. She carried the weight of the family finances squarely upon her shoulders, and they were not young, strong shoulders any longer. She spent her days surrounded by beautiful things, keeping house for a cultured, self-made, successful man. She returned home each night to a lazy drunk who was usually asleep in his split-out, stinking recliner in front of a blaring television.

The old-school attitude that she could not seem to shake would not allow her to leave him, however. The scandal of divorce was greater than the scandal of alcoholism. If she left him, people would blame her for not making him happy. Yet by staying with him, she was miserable. "If only I just had a little more money," she sighed. "I wouldn't give none of it to Whipple. I wouldn't even tell him. I'd save it up for a nicer place to live. I'd go to one of them nice restaurants and have myself a fifty-dollah lobstah." She stopped scrubbing and leaned against the marble counter. "Maybe I should ask Mr. Harriman for a raise. It's been much as a year now, I think. Yes, that's just what I'll do." She looked through the kitchen door and into the hallway, remembering the conversation between Harriman and his brother. "Guess I'll just wait a little minute before I bring up money, though."

She thought for another long moment. Thinking did not come easily for Jane Whipple. But then she smiled. She rinsed off the sink, opened the refrigerator, and began to prepare what she knew to be Joshua Harriman's favorite lunch.

℞

James Harriman had walked up the hill to his brother's house. Now he quickly strode back down in anger. He jaywalked across the first intersection, not even seeing the car that screeched to a halt just in time for him to pass. He marched back to his tiny office with its view of the brick wall of the adjacent building a dozen feet away, and slammed the door. "Bastard!" he spat aloud, throwing himself into his chair. "What makes him think he's so damned self-righteous just because he's got more money? He never even married! Never bothered to have a child! Wanted to keep it all to himself!"

James sat with his head in his hands for several seconds. His own business selling insurance had never been very lucrative. He earned a decent living, but he certainly had little respect in the profession. His only major client at this point was the Maine Museum of Art and that was thanks to Joshua, of course.

James stood and paced back and forth across the room. He was a weak man, and an envious one. The combination did not work well. He blamed everyone else for his troubles. His wife. His daughter. His brother. James Harriman was never responsible for James Harriman's problems. It was always some other force acting upon him. As he grew older he found himself increasingly angry with his life and blamed everyone else all the more. Especially Joshua. Perfect, rich, powerful Joshua. It was enough to drive him insane. Every time he asked his brother for money, Joshua made him feel smaller and smaller. Couldn't Josh see that it was not his fault?

That did not help the current situation. No, he needed to find a way for his daughter to get her tuition bill settled. He knew that she probably needed far more than what she had requested. This was just a temporary, stopgap measure. The forthcoming tuition bill was only an excuse. Her lifestyle was astronomical, just like her mother's. She could have lived off the interest of her trust fund if she had been careful. Instead she squandered it on trips to Paris and London and Florence, along with expensive clothes and apartments.

James Harriman looked down at his shoes, showing years of wear after being resoled three times. "Maybe Josh is right on one score," he muttered. "Maybe it is time I put my foot down when it comes to those two women." Then he shook his head knowing that he could never carry it through.

ℏ

Dan Chambers stood on the deck of his boat coiling a line. He looped the rope under with his right hand, then caught it in his left in a smooth, rhythmic motion. He could not remember the first time he had done this. *'Dad taught me, I'm sure,'* he thought. He looked across the dock as he continued his work and saw a familiar person walking toward him. Dan stopped, shaded his eyes from the glare, and then waved at the figure.

Tom Cole waved back. He walked up to the boat as Dan tied off the line. "Not going out today?" Tom asked.

"Nope. Storms this afternoon, or so they say. Plus, I have to do a little work here, and," he looked up and grinned, "I have to get to the grocery store and buy food."

"That'd be kinda important," said Tom.

"Yeah. Can't ever seem to find the time for it either, usually. Spend way too much money eating out."

Tom laughed. "I know that one." He looked over at the boat longingly. "My family lobsters, you know. For a living. Except me."

"Do you ever wish you were doing that?"

Tom gazed out across the water. "Sometimes," he said quietly.

Dan looked at him quizzically. Something was on Tom's mind, but he did not know him well enough to inquire. *'He'll sort it out,'* thought Dan.

"Do you ever need a hand? On the weekends, maybe?" asked Tom.

"Yeah, sometimes. Can I keep you in mind?"

"That'd be great. It'd be good to do something on the water other than haul traps. Might be a whole new career option."

Dan laughed. "What? And give up the lucrative world of art? Doesn't my sister pay you well enough?"

Tom smiled. "Well enough. Considering I'm just an intern. But I like to get outside, too. I'm glad the museum is on the water. At least I can look out the window." He shoved his hands in the pockets of his khakis. "I'm just not sure what I'm doing with my life. Guess I've got career options, but I can't figure out which one is the right one."

Dan looked up at the museum, then back at Tom. "How'd you get caught up there in the first place?"

"It was funny, really," Tom replied. "I was a launch driver at Portland Yacht Club last summer. I did it a couple of days a week to earn some extra cash. This gray haired rich guy, although that describes nearly everyone there," he stopped when Dan snorted a laugh, "This guy went out to his boat all the time and we just started talking. I didn't know it then, but he was Joshua Harriman. He asked if I was in school and what I was studying. I told him, and then it felt like he was quizzing me. He asked me a ton of questions about artists, sculptors, architects. I guess I passed, because one day he showed up and handed me an application for the internship position. I was surprised, but not nearly as much as when I actually got the job."

"That doesn't happen every day. Most folks search weeks, months…"

"I know. I'm pretty lucky. Still don't know what I really want to do for a career, though. I like this art stuff, and I'm good at it, but I don't know if I can dedicate my life to it."

Dan nodded. He had never dreamed as a child that he would be taking tourists on laps around the bay for a living. But he liked his life. "You know, you just have to like what you're doing from one twenty-four hours to the next. I'm convinced that's all that really matters." He glanced at the cooler on the deck. "Sun's almost past the yardarm. You on your lunch break?"

"Yup."

"Want a beer?"

"Thought you'd never ask," said Tom.

Dan grinned and pulled out two cold cans from the cooler on the deck. He handed one to Tom. They both opened them with a loud crack. "Cheers," he said with mock sincerity and the two drank. "Have a seat," said Dan.

They sat on the blue wooden seats of the boat's open deck in the warm sun, looking out at the glistening bay. A harbor seal popped its shiny black face out of the water and goggled back at them for a moment before disappearing again.

Tom chuckled. "They look human almost, don't they?" he said.

"Yup. I can just picture those sailors of old, half drunk, half starved, thinking they were mermaids. Anything must have looked good to them after weeks at sea."

"Can't imagine being out that long. Once I went out for a week with one of my brothers on a commercial boat. We were part of a five-man crew. By the third day, I thought I'd lose my mind. You start hearing the same stories over and over. Plus the smell wasn't very pretty, either, and I'm not talking about the fish."

"Yikes. Hope the pay was good."

"That was the worst of it," said Tom. "We'd agreed to go for a cut of the profits. They usually haul in about $5,000 so I'd have made a grand in a week. Well, on the fifth day the refrigeration unit conked out. Lost nearly half of what we'd caught already and had to go in to port for repairs. Took us the better part of a day just to get back. Never been on such a silent boat before. We were all really mad." He shook his head.

Dan groaned. "I can see why you're considering other careers." He looked around the deck of his boat. "I never dreamed I'd be doing this, but I do like it. I like people. The extravert of the family. Dulcie's the introvert."

"Really?" said Tom, looking surprised. "She doesn't seem it."

"Watch her at a party. She doesn't mingle much."

Tom thought back to the opening of the Homer exhibit. "You know, you're right. It's odd. I was having reservations about this art museum career because I'm not much of a people person, but I guess I don't need to be, entirely?"

Dan to a long swig of beer. "Don't know. Dulcie has to deal with a lot of different people. You should talk with her about it. I know she'd be happy to give you some advice. Tell her I sent you."

"I'll tell her you were acting as my career counselor," Tom said.

Dan rolled his eyes. "Now that would probably get you more advice than you bargained for!" he replied.

Tom tipped his head back and drank the last of his beer while it was still cold. "Guess I'd better get something solid in me before I head back in. Wouldn't want the boss to think I only had a liquid lunch." He thanked Dan for the beverage and wandered back up the dock toward Commercial Street.

When he reached the sidewalk he stopped, looking back and forth. He didn't know which direction he should go. A gust of wind caught his tie and sent it flipping over his shoulder. He quickly reached for it and slid it back in front of him. He was very careful of his ties. He owned exactly three, all of which his mother had bought for him before he started the internship. "You gotta look professional," she had said with pride. He knew she really did not have the money to spare for them. "They're polyester, so you can clean 'em if you need to. That silk looks nice, but it don't clean good." She showed him how to tie one, and made him practice until he got it right.

How she knew the proper way to knot a tie was a mystery to Tom. He had never known of his parents attending even a semi-formal function in his life. He knew his father certainly didn't own any ties. No reason to.

His mother was smart, in her own way. She had common sense. His father was another story. He was a hard worker and a gentle soul, but could never seem to get ahead. His world was limited. Everyone said that he had been handsome in his day, and certainly that had something to do with why Tom's mother had married him. Looks generally fade, though. And they usually can't pay the bills. Not for long, anyway.

Tom worried about his mother. Increasingly, she looked older than her age. He knew that her joints had started to ache. She refused to see a doctor, making light of his concern. Tom knew she only did that in an attempt to keep him from being insistent.

His mother had given up so much, especially for him. When Tom was finishing high school, something his brothers had not done, she had made him apply to college. He had wanted to work so that he could contribute to the family finances. She stubbornly refused to let him, saying that he could earn far more if he would just spend a few years getting a degree. Of course she was right, but he still felt guilty. He applied for every scholarship that he could, and managed to cover his entire tuition. That had made him feel better.

The scent of something cooking jarred him from his thoughts. It was an outdoor hotdog stand. *'Perfect,'* thought Tom. *'A decent lunch, and not expensive.'* He walked up toward the vendor and was about to order two hot dogs, then thought better of it and just got one. That way, he still had money for one more the next day. He covered it with relish and mustard, then turned back toward the museum, eating as he walked, careful to keep his tie clean.

CHAPTER 4

Dulcie got out of bed, stretched, and pulled open the blue and white striped curtain over the window. She groaned. The morning was cloudy and threatened rain. '*Dan will not be happy about this,*' she thought, '*but I'll have a busy day.*' She showered, listened to the weather forecast, then put on a light cotton dress. She clipped her still-damp hair back with a large tortoise-shell barrette. It was warm for May; the forecast said the temperatures would be well into the eighties. This was the oppressive type of heat that usually waited until at least July. It made her head ache. "Damn," she swore softly. "I really need to focus today."

Arriving at the museum half an hour later, Dulcie slowly sipped her coffee. She reviewed the files that she had failed to even remove from her briefcase the night before. A sound in the doorway caused her to jump; she nearly spilled coffee on her dress.

"Hey! Sorry about that! Didn't mean to sneak up on you!" exclaimed Mr. Harriman.

Dulcie smiled. "I am very happy to see you. You may sneak up any time you wish. Please, sit down! I was just about to refill my coffee. Would you like some too?"

"I'd like nothing better. Regular, if you please."

Dulcie left the room for a moment, then returned with two sturdy, steaming, heavy white mugs. "I'm very glad that you dropped by," she said. "I think that we finally have the money now for the Homer. The donations were good and there's enough left in the budget. However, if the bidding runs high…."

"Which it invariably does," he interjected.

"Yes, which it always does, do you think that we could obtain any additional funds from you to cover the difference?"

"What do you project the difference to be?"

"It could be as much as fifty thousand."

"Is that all?"

Dulcie grinned.

"I will be happy to provide a donation if required, but on one condition."

"Name it," said Dulcie, stopping her cup half way to her lips.

"I haven't been down to Christie's in ages. I'd like to go to New York and do the bidding myself, if that's all right with you. I'm getting to be an old man, and need a little excitement now and then."

Dulcie laughed. "Mr. Harriman, don't be silly! You are not an old man, and you can certainly do the bidding! In fact, that would help us to save a little money on the fee if we had a representative there to handle it. So you see, you help us economically in many ways!"

"Great. Then it's settled. What's the estimate?"

"My research shows that it should go for roughly $350,000. We have a little over $325,000 in donations, and another twenty-five in the budget reserved for it right now. However, last week there was a small bidding war for one of Homer's Bahamas watercolors, so there could be someone out there who really wants ours, too."

"Do you have any idea who it was?"

"Not a clue. It was an anonymous telephone bidder and I haven't been able to get in touch with my usual auction house contacts to get any of the inside scoop. I'll keep trying, but you may easily be on your own down there."

"All right, we'll see what happens. Should be exciting!"

"Very! I'll copy all of the information that you may need, and have someone drop it by later today." Dulcie knew that Mr. Harriman was not well versed in opening digital files or even reading email. "Will you be at home this afternoon?"

"Certainly. Looks like rain, so I think I'll stay off the boat until the weekend." Mr. Harriman frowned at the window.

"Good idea. How's she handling these days?"

"Like a dream. I had her keel scraped last week, and she flies now. You should bring some friends and come try her out."

"I'll do that! Thanks! Oh, and I'll probably talk with you later today, but good luck in New York."

"Thank you, dear. Everything will be just fine. Wait and see." He smiled, put his empty coffee cup on her desk and left the room whistling softly.

'He always whistles when he's nervous,' Dulcie thought. 'He told me that once. A habit he can't seem to break. Wonder what he could possibly be nervous about? He's bid on tons of artworks before at auction.' She shrugged her shoulders, clearing away all thoughts of Joshua Harriman, and refocused on her work.

℞

Joshua Harriman walked briskly down Commercial Street, parallel to the ocean. The wharves extended out from it far into the water. In the past century, sailing ships could pull forward so far alongside the wharves that their bowsprits extended over the street for several feet. Now many of the wharves had been filled in or built over, and docking ships generally stayed on the far ends.

While he walked, Mr. Harriman's head jerked up and down as he considered various thoughts. When he contemplated, his head dropped. When he arrived at a solution, it came up. When a new problem occurred to him, his chin was on his chest again. He looked as though he was trying to avoid all the bowsprits that would have blocked his way had he walked that street a century earlier.

He felt a little odd. 'It's this storm coming upon us,' he thought. 'A new project is just what I need to get my mind off my troubles. This adventure in New York will do the trick. I'll just pop down there, pick up the Homer, and pop back.' He smiled at the idea.

He turned and walked to the end of a wharf. The islands were barely visible in the bay. Joshua Harriman loved to sail the coast of Maine. It was rough, rocky, and difficult to navigate. It kept its secrets. Mapmakers said that if you could straighten it out, it would extend from Nova Scotia to Florida. That was a lot of secrets.

The letter he had received the day before was one of them. He sighed and stuffed his hands deeper into his pockets, bobbing his head down for several moments, then up once again. '*Not much I can do about it now,*' he thought. '*Some people just can't leave well enough alone. Why would anyone want to bring up old trouble when things are working out all right as they are?*' He tried to put the letter out of his mind. Still, it made him nervous.

He thought about his brother. His head went down. Damned fool. He'll bail her out again for sure. Wonder how he'll pull it off, though. I suppose I should help him, but best to let him stew for a while. Maybe he'll develop a spine in the process.

He turned away from the ocean and walked back to Commercial Street, continuing down it, still deep in thought, until he ran nearly headlong into the subject of his brooding. "Greetings, James!" he said, hoping his voice covered his negative mood. He stuck out his hand. The other man sighed and shook it. "How is everything?"

James Harriman sighed again. "Look, Josh. I'm sorry I came to you about the money. I know you're right. They need to learn and I'm the only one that can teach them, I suppose. I'm just afraid that it's too late." He kicked a tiny rock down the brick sidewalk in front of him.

Joshua looked at his brother's shoes. '*Worn,*' he thought. His tie was stained as well. Joshua's heart went out to his brother, but he didn't want to give in entirely. He looked at his brother and said quietly, "Whom shall I make out the check to?"

James looked away. "Never mind."

Joshua put his hand on his brother's shoulder. "Look. I happen to have a great deal of money just by the sheer luck of the draw. I love my business and that's my success. I help out my own, no matter what." He pulled out his checkbook and wrote in it. "There," he said tearing out a fresh check. "I've made it out to you, and there's some extra for your ulcer." James smiled halfheartedly and shoved it in his breast pocket.

"Thanks. I'll do better. I mean…well, thanks," he said and quickly turned and walked away.

'Damn,' thought Joshua. 'What else can I do? I can't fix his screwed-up affairs. I can't feel guilty because his life didn't turn out as nicely as mine did. It just takes lots of hard work. I'm getting his daughter started on a good career. At least he has a daughter….' He shook his head as if to clear away any more unwelcome thoughts of regret toward the past and began to whistle as he continued down the street.

The rest of the day was muggy and blustery. Joshua Harriman had returned home to examine his wine cellar. Mrs. Whipple heard him come in. She had small beads of sweat on her upper lip, due in part to her exertions with the vacuum but also to her current state of mind. She had not asked her employer for a raise the previous day. The timing did not seem to be right. Today the task was imperative.

Arriving at home the night before she had seen a strange car in the driveway. Hurrying in the back door of the house she caught the end of an argument in the next room.

"Look, Jed, I can't hold 'em off any longer. You give it to me tomorrow!"

"Yeah, yeah. Don't worry. I'll take care of it."

Both men had been silent when Jane Whipple noisily closed the back door behind her. "Jed? We got company?" she had called out from the kitchen.

"Nope. Just an old friend from work stopped by," her husband replied. She heard the front door open and close, then saw the car pull out of the driveway. Jed Whipple came into the kitchen, walked straight to the refrigerator, and pulled out a beer. "What's for supper?" he asked after a huge swig. She had glared at him for a long moment, then left the room without a word to hang up her jacket. She knew he would be going through her purse while her back was turned. She lingered in the hallway, letting him take what he needed. She didn't have the strength to argue with him.

Now, as she switched off the vacuum and collected its cord, she thought about what she would say to Mr. Harriman. She had thought about concocting a story about a sick relative, but knew that he was far more clever and would most likely see right through it. No, the direct approach was the best in this case. She lugged the vacuum into the pantry, took off her apron, wiped her face with it, and put it on the counter. She stood as straight as her aching back would allow and marched into Mr. Harriman's office.

"Sir?" she said with an unsteady voice.

"Yes, Jane?" Mr. Harriman smiled and looked at her over the top of the paper that he was reading.

"Sir, I need to speak with you as my employer." She took a deep breath. "I've worked with you for much as a year now, and I hope that you've been pleased with everythin' that I've done...."

"Good God, Jane! You're not giving notice, are you? You're the best housekeeper I've ever had around here!"

Mrs. Whipple smiled, encouraged. "Thank you, sir. No, I'm not givin' no notice. What I'm doin' is, well, I'm requestin' a raise. I think I've proven my worth." Yes, that was good, she thought. She had proven her worth.

Mr. Harriman deliberately put down the newspaper. He was seated in a leather wingback chair by the empty fireplace and gestured for Mrs. Whipple to sit in the one opposite. She perched on the edge, crumpling a cotton handkerchief nervously in her hands.

"Mrs. Whipple, I couldn't agree more. Did you have a particular sum in mind?"

"Well, I didn't…, well…, no, sir, I hadn't thought of how much…."

"Why don't you let me think about the amount then, and we can talk about it again on Monday morning. I'm going out of town for a couple of days, but I'll be back for the weekend and will look at the household accounts then. Would that be all right?"

"Why, yes! Yes, it would! You see, my husband is out of work, and we just…." She looked as though she would burst into tears at any moment.

Mr. Harriman stood and put his hand on her shoulder. "Yes, it is a difficult time, I know. Why don't you take the rest of the day off? A little holiday." He pulled out his wallet and handed her a one-hundred dollar bill. "Treat yourself to lunch, too."

A tear escaped and rolled down her ruddy, plump cheek as she nodded, taking the money. She sniffed loudly and grunted something that sounded like a thank-you as she hurried from the room. Mr. Harriman shook his head. *'Poor thing,'* he thought. *'She's just tired out. It's this oppressive heat.'*

CHAPTER 5

On Thursday morning Dulcie arrived at her office early. She closed the door quietly behind her and sat down at her large oak desk. Then she spun around full circle in her chair several times and thought about the Homer. "What would I do without Mr. Harriman?" she exclaimed. She was almost giddy from the spinning. Gripping the desk quickly on her fourth lap around, she stopped herself.

She dreaded the wait. It was the worst part. Weeks, often months, of research and planning could go into the decision to buy a work. Then it all came down to one moment. *'Like a horse race,'* she thought. Would they have the highest bid? For once, Dulcie was nearly sure that they would. She heard tapping at the door. "Come in!" she called, trying to sound composed.

Tom opened the door and entered looking a little shabby, as usual. *'He's so intelligent,'* thought Dulcie, *'but he just doesn't pay attention to the common sense things.'* On this particular morning Tom had neglected to fasten two buttons on his shirt under his necktie. Even at this early hour of the day the tie had sunk into the now open space between buttons and buttonholes. His shirttail trailed along behind him, sadly rumpled. Dulcie looked again at the tie. *'Funny,'* she thought. *'No matter what the rest of his clothes look like, that tie is always perfect.'* She smiled.

Tom dragged a hand through his curly hair, a habit that Dulcie had quickly learned to equate with a question about to be asked. "Yes, Tom?"

"Well, here's the situation. I need to head back home for the weekend. My Dad is sick, and my brothers need help with the boat. It's a full moon and the lobsters are making tracks. Really great hauls. Would it be all right if I take Friday afternoon off and help them? I'm finishing my final write-up on my research today. I can give it to you by five o'clock.

"Tom, that would be fine. Is your Dad all right?"

"Yup. Just the flu."

"Oh no! That's too bad. I hope he's better soon."

"Yeah, I'm sure he will be. The doctor has him on a whole bunch of stuff which he hates taking, Mom says."

Dulcie grimaced. "Good, but you be careful out there," she said, remembering the times that her brother and father were out on the ocean.

"I'll just be happy not to put on a tie for a few days." He grinned and looked down. Seeing the buttons undone he rolled his eyes, turned pink, and quickly fixed his shirt. Dulcie laughed.

"Tom," said Dulcie, "all of your brothers are lobstermen except you?"

"Yup. Mom has a theory about me. She thinks I was switched at birth."

"No!" Dulcie's eyes widened. "Not seriously?"

Tom laughed. "Maybe. She says," he cleared his throat and his voice increased an octave, "I was in the hospital, you know, and this other lady, she come in screamin' in labor, just like me, 'cept I wasn't screamin' cause I'd been through it twice already and just popped this thurd one roit out. She was some lawyuh or somethin' and looked wicked rich and wicked smahht. I thought she must be the kinda lady to have a wicked smahht kid. When my Tommy got older and went to school, he just had a wicked head for learnin', so I figure I got that rich lady's kid and my dumb kid must be livin' with them rich folks someplace now." His voice dropped to its usual soft, low tone again. "That's the story she tells."

Dulcie laughed. "You don't believe it's true, do you?"

He shrugged his shoulders. "Who could know? I mean, I guess we could do a DNA test or something, but it wouldn't change anything."

Dulcie only shook her head and smiled. "Stranger things have happened."

"Yup. Seriously, though, Mom and Dad do need my help this weekend. It's all right if I leave early tomorrow?"

"Of course. My father was a fisherman. I know what it means to lose a day's catch. If you can get me the report this afternoon, I'll bring it home with me tonight and read it, then we can talk about it in the morning. You can leave as soon as we're done. How does that sound?"

"Sound's perfect. I'll call my brother. Thanks!" He quickly left her office.

Dulcie liked Tom. He worked hard. "I think I'll reward him," she thought. "When we get the Homer, I'll put him in charge of researching a new exhibit. The small one of the local artists. It will look very good on his resume." Then she smiled slyly, thinking, "It will also make Alicia spit like a cat!"

ଔ

At ten o'clock Dulcie's phone rang.

"Dr. Chambers," spoke the saccharine voice, "it's Alicia Harriman. I'm running into a bit of a snag here in Boston. It seems the curator's files are a little mixed up and it's taking more time than expected. Would it be all right if I stayed down here for one more night, and not come back to the museum tomorrow as planned?"

Dulcie hesitated for a moment. She suspected that Alicia was lying and that she simply wanted to enjoy the big city a bit more. Dulcie had no patience for her during this week especially, however. She decided to let Alicia get away with it. This time.

"Sure, Alicia. Do what you need to do. I'll need your information first thing on Monday morning, though."

"Of course," Alicia replied with a hint of condescension.

Annoyed, Dulcie decided to give her a little scare. "Perhaps I should send Tom down this afternoon so he can help you out tomorrow?" She asked.

"Oh no, no, no! Nothing I can't handle! Really!" Alicia exclaimed, the sweetness gone from her voice.

"All right. I'll see you on Monday, then." Dulcie could almost hear Alicia's relieved sigh as she hung up the phone.

'That girl is trouble,' thought Dulcie. 'Too much like her mother, from what I've heard Mr. Harriman say.'

Dulcie continued her own work that afternoon with difficulty. Periodically she stared out the window. At four o'clock she abandoned all efforts and turned to the day's newspapers. She pulled out the Boston Globe and opened it to the Arts section. Nothing very exciting. She leafed through the pages, quickly scanning the columns. A brief story caught her eye about a recent theft. "Hmm," she muttered, "another small item from a small museum." The New England art community had been hearing about this for nearly two years. Some clever person had devised a way to steal small works of art from less secure museums and storage locations. So far they had been quite successful.

The latest heist had been a miniature nineteenth century portrait painted by one of the Peale family members. The two Peale brothers, Charles Willson and

James, had been enormously talented. Charles had intended that his children would follow, ostentatiously naming them after the great masters: Titian, Rembrandt, and Raphaelle. James had fathered two daughters, Anna and Sarah, who became respected artists as well. The stolen work was a miniature by Anna and, once again following the pattern of the other thefts, it was not as valuable as the works done by the fathers or the sons. This thief certainly knew art and knew what would sell quickly with few questions.

"Now that's the smart way to lead a life of crime," said Dulcie aloud. Many small museums lacked sufficient security for their less valuable items, especially items in storage rooms. She knew from experience that it would be quite easy in some museums to slip out with something. Generally no one would miss it until weeks, months, perhaps even years later.

The black market thrived in the art world. Private collectors often chose to acquire works through private dealers. They sometimes did not question the source, especially if the price was right. Private collectors were becoming increasingly knowledgeable, Dulcie had noticed. Authenticity and provenance were not issues of concern for many of them; they were experts in their own right and knew well enough when a work was genuine. Of course thieves and forgers were also becoming quite good at faking provenance documents as well. New technology made it surprisingly easy.

She read through the article. The most recent theft had been from the museum at the Augusta Academy in Cambridge. Dulcie had been there a couple of months before with Tom and Alicia. *'They didn't have much security,'* she thought. *'Just one alarm system at night, plus that guard.'* She remembered how Alicia had eyed the tall, handsome guard coyly. "She's just awful," she said aloud.

"Who is awful?"

Dulcie jumped. Tom had walked in silently while she was reading.

"Oh. No one. Just someone I read about." She looked down feeling her face grow warm.

"Hey, I read about that this morning," said Tom, pointing at the art theft story. "Somebody has a system."

"Yes. It has to be an insider, too. What do you think?"

Tom nodded. "Has to be. They can get into storage areas. They know which things to take. Small things, moderate value, stuff that won't get noticed very soon. They must have connections, too, so that they can get rid of the goods."

Dulcie grinned. " 'Get rid of the goods?' You've been watching too much TV, Tom!"

"Well, it's true! They do need to get rid of what they take. Quickly, too!"

"You're right, of course. I wonder if it's anyone I know?"

"I'll bet it is. Most of the thefts have been around Boston and north. They haven't hit Maine yet, have they?"

"Not to my knowledge. And they won't, if I can help it! Not here, anyway."

Tom looked back down at the article and chuckled. "You know, I've always thought that if I were ever to lead a life of crime, I would counterfeit one dollar bills."

Dulcie raised an eyebrow but said nothing.

"No, I am not planning a career change, but when you think about it, counterfeiters usually make twenties or more, right?"

"I'm not an authority on the subject, but that's what you generally hear about," she replied.

"Well, I would make ones. No one would suspect that a one-dollar bill is a fake. Think about how many you spend in a week. Buy a cup of coffee. Get a sandwich for lunch. You could pass off bad ones all over the place!"

"And they'd add up after a while, I suppose," Dulcie mused.

"Right! It wouldn't be the big time, but it would help lighten the load. I mean, you couldn't quit your day job, but that's good because then no one would suspect."

Dulcie was laughing now. "And, if you did get caught, the judge would be lenient because it's such a ridiculous notion!"

Tom grinned. "I swear it would work!"

"Yes, well let me know how it turns out."

Tom looked a bit sheepish. He decided to change the subject. "Anyway, here's the report I promised." He handed her a folder. "Enjoy!"

"Thank you, Tom. We'll talk about it tomorrow morning. Then you're free to go help your family."

"Thanks," he said. "Have a good night."

"You too, Tom."

The telephone rang at the front desk of the museum, just outside Dulcie's office. The museum was shifting to its evening staff, a much smaller group of part-time assistants who often trickled in a bit late after working daytime jobs. Dulcie let it ring twice, and then answered it at her own extension. "Maine Museum of Art. May I help you?"

"Dulcie? That you?" Joshua Harriman's voice sounded crackly.

"Yes! Can you hear me all right?" she said loudly.

"Good enough! I'm on my cell phone. Guess I oughta pay my bill!" he laughed. "Just wanted you to know I'm in New York now! At the Waldorf, or I hope to be as soon as this damned traffic lets up! Got the best cab driver in New York, though! Right, Lenny?" Dulcie heard a man laugh in the background.

'He *must have had a scotch or two on the flight down*,' she thought. "All right, Mr. Harriman!" she shouted. "Is there anything more that you need from us up here?"

"Nope! Just calling to see if you have last minute instructions for me! I'll be off to the auction in the morning. You've got my cell phone number, right?"

"Right!"

"OK, call if you need to! Otherwise, I'm bringin' home a Homer!" he exploded with laughter at his quip.

Dulcie laughed too. "Good one! Have a nice dinner, and call me when you have the painting!"

"Roger Willco! Over and out!"

"Bye!"

Dulcie hung up the phone while shaking her head. "That man can be a total fool!" she thought out loud.

The mention of dinner made her realize how hungry she was. Scooping up Tom's report and several other files, she stuffed them into her worn leather briefcase and strode out the door, wishing the evening staff a good night on her way.

An onshore breeze greeted her with cool air. The sun sank slowly toward the horizon. She paused for a moment feeling the warm sun and the misty air at the same time. '*I love this place,*' she thought for the hundredth time. She was jarred from her thoughts by a police car, sirens blaring, roaring down the street. Dulcie shivered as she watched it continue on. She pulled the collar of her dress more tightly around her neck and walked home.

CHAPTER 6

Fog can roll in within seconds on the ocean. Sailors find themselves in view of land one moment, and unable to see the bow of their own ship the next. Friday morning was one of the most perfect examples of this that Dulcie had ever seen. As she walked down the street, the fog enveloped her. She had been looking ahead toward the art museum when it suddenly disappeared.

Dulcie hoped that her brother had chosen to stay in for the morning. She remembered when she was a little girl waiting by the radio to hear her father's voice from his boat. On foggy days her mother worried. Tankers easily slipped into and out of the harbor and could loom over a small fishing vessel in the fog with no warning. Dulcie remembered holding the cold microphone of their radio transmitter in her hand, pressing the button, and saying, as calmly as she could,

"Nora May, Nora May, come in Nora May." Then she would wait. Sometimes she heard nothing, and would try again several times within the hour. When at last she heard her father's voice saying, "This is the Nora May. That you, Dulcie? Over!" they were the most beautiful words in the world.

A chill ran through her, in spite of her trench coat. Dulcie turned into a small cafe for breakfast. She began to take off her coat, but then thought better of it. She walked up to the counter and ordered an egg sandwich and a cup of tea to go. The waitress brought the tea while Dulcie waited, and she sipped it while staring moodily at the fog.

"Nice day, huh?" the waitress quipped.

"Ugh," replied Dulcie.

"We'll be busy, though. No one out on the water today 'cept fools. Got my tip jar primed and waitin' right he-ya," she grinned.

"Stay one step ahead of 'em. That's the best ploy," said Dulcie.

"You got that right, dee-uh!" she replied. "Here's your sandwich. Have a good mornin'!"

"Thanks. You too," said Dulcie and tossed a dollar into the jar.

Five minutes later she was in her office. She could concentrate on nothing. Her head ached again. She slowly nibbled away at her egg sandwich. *'What's wrong with me?'* she thought.

She met with Tom. He kept looking out the window as they talked. At last, when they were finished, he said, "I don't like this fog. Could be local, but it looks like it might go all the way up to Brunswick, too."

"Can you still go out in it, Tom?"

"Yeah, we've got a GPS. Plus, my brother navigates off the charts really well. He always knows where we are. It's like a sixth sense with him."

"Well, be careful anyway."

"I will." Tom glanced outside again, then left the room.

ℓ

Detective Nicholas Black sat at his usual table in the coffee shop, a block away from the police station, absorbed in a large book. He did not hear his partner as he approached the table.

"Whatcha readin'?" boomed Johnson.

Nick tried to close the book and slide it into the seat next to him, but his partner quickly snatched it away. He could move surprisingly fast for such a large man. "What have we here? *The History of American Art.*" He looked at Nick over the top of the book with mock sincerity. "Doing a bit of homework, are we?"

Nick took the book away firmly. "Just trying to expand my horizons a little, that's all." He looked out the window as his face grew red.

Johnson decided to let the issue rest for the moment. "Well, I think I'll expand my waistline a little. Back in a minute." He headed for the pastry counter.

Nick found his place in the book again and marked it with a paper napkin. Then he put it on the seat beside him and draped his jacket over it. He stood and joined Johnson.

"Having a treat as well? I'm going for the apple strudel myself."

Nick shook his head. "Nope. Just another coffee."

"Ayuh. Best for you to stay in shape, I guess. For the ladies. As for me, I'm a happily married man, and it shows." He patted his stomach. The waitress behind the counter giggled.

Nick took his coffee back to the table and waited for Johnson. "So, any good cases brewing?" He asked as his partner sat down.

"Nope. I'm down to organizing the files on that damned computer now. You know I'm desperate when I start doing that."

"Yes, you've always been so computer literate. I remember you fought against having one for the longest time. You were the last holdout."

"Yeah, yeah. I'm gettin' used to it. Just don't make me use one of those dumb hand-held things that people are always poking at."

"Come on! Those are great for a crime scene! You can take notes on them!"

"No way. You go ahead with it, buddy. I'll stick with my trusty note pad." He patted his breast pocket.

"Well, it's all irrelevant at the moment anyway," said Nick. "We need a case before we can start taking notes on anything."

Johnson took a big bite of strudel and chewed thoughtfully. "Summer's nigh upon us. Somethin's brewin'. I can feel it."

Nick rolled his eyes. "The detective's intuition, again?"

"You mock me, but you'll learn!" said Johnson, pointing at his partner with his fork. "Although, maybe you don't want a case just yet. You've got homework to do before you ask somebody out on a date. Am I right?"

"Shut up," replied Nick. He stood, grabbing his book and jacket. "Enjoy the strudel. See you back at the station."

Johnson watched him leave. "Whew! Stuck a nerve there!" he thought aloud, and smiled.

℘

For the remainder of the day each time the phone rang Dulcie jumped. At last, late in the afternoon, the much anticipated call came through.

"Dulcie, it's all ours!" Mr. Harriman said.

She grinned. "How much? No, don't tell me. Just tell me if you had to dip into your own funds."

"Let's just say I have yet another excellent tax write-off this year. I'll be back tonight, but late. I'm booked on a nine o-clock flight into Portland. Can I bring it around to the museum tomorrow morning? I'll keep it at the house overnight. Will you get in touch with Jim to make sure that we're set on the insurance business for transit?"

"Of course! Give me a call in the morning when you're up, and I'll meet you here. Thank you so much!"

"My pleasure, dear."

Dulcie exhaled heavily with relief. They had it! She walked into the main gallery and looked at the empty spot on the wall. *'Tomorrow, everything will be complete,'* she thought.

CHAPTER 7

Saturday was clear and sunny. The fog of the previous day had burned away. Dulcie woke early, waiting for Mr. Harriman's call. By ten o'clock the phone was still silent. At ten-thirty she decided to call him. She reached only his voicemail and left a quick message.

By noon, Dulcie still had heard nothing from Mr. Harriman. She was beginning to feel a little frantic. She hated the transit phases with a new work.

'I'll drive out to his house. He was probably up late last night and just got a slow start today,' thought Dulcie. She grabbed her keys and jumped into her old Jeep Wrangler, then made her way through the winding streets. As she drove, she thought she saw Tom. She nearly waved to him, but caught herself. *No, he's in*

Brunswick this weekend. It's just somebody who looks like him. She thought about him out on the water. "At least he has a good day for hauling traps," she said aloud.

Mr. Harriman's elaborately detailed Victorian mansion sat on the Western Promenade, an elegant residential section of Portland, overlooking the salt marshes of the Fore River below. On a clear day the view extended for miles.

Dulcie slowed as she drove along, always admiring the beautiful homes. The district was a lesson in residential architecture, with examples of Classical Revival, Victorian, Italianate, Shingle Style, Gothic, and many more all within walking distance of each other. Several had been designed by the noted nineteenth century architect John Calvin Stevens. Dulcie had wandered the streets many times.

A soft, cool breeze sweet with salt blew up from the marshes. Dulcie parked in the paved drive of Mr. Harriman's house, jumped out, and quickly walked up the front path. Before reaching the door she paused, taking a deep breath of the wonderful air. The windows of the house were open, and she heard someone talking loudly on the telephone. As she hesitated, she recognized the housekeeper's voice.

"Whipple! I told you to stay away from the track! ... How much did you lose this time? ...Well, it's twice as much as last! How do you think we're gonna pay for... wait, someone's here. I'll talk to you later. Don't you leave home, and don't you call nobody!"

Dulcie waited for a moment longer. She was a little embarrassed to have overheard the conversation, and tried to pretend that she had not. She rang the bell, and Mrs. Whipple let her in, saying that she had only just arrived herself. "I ain't caught sight o' Mr. Harriman yet. The door was unlocked, so I expect he maybe went for a walk."

"The door was unlocked?" Dulcie said in surprise. "Could I look around for a moment? Mr. Harriman brought home a very expensive painting last night. I need to get it to the museum."

"Sure thing. Come in. Have a look 'round. Prob'ly in his study. I'll be back in here," she said, nodding her head toward the kitchen.

Dulcie's mind was spinning. The door was unlocked? Something was not right. She nearly ran across the living room and into the study. She did not see Mr. Harriman or the painting. She ran back to the living room, looking for a box that would be the right size to hold the Homer. Nothing was there.

Dulcie thought that perhaps he had left a note in his study, or something that would indicate where he had gone. She returned to the room and hurried over to Mr. Harriman's desk. Half way around it she froze. "Jane!" she screamed.

Two feet were sticking out from behind the desk, lying completely still beside the ornately carved mahogany.

The housekeeper hurried into the room. "Jane, I think that something is very wrong. I don't dare look."

Mrs. Whipple was beside her, staring at the feet. "I don't dare either, Miss," she whispered.

"Please call an ambulance, and the police!" Dulcie said, although Mrs. Whipple was already running toward the door, heading for the telephone.

Dulcie slowly stepped around the desk. It was indeed Mr. Harriman lying on the floor, staring back at her blankly. One side of his handsome face was perfectly intact, but the other was marred by a large gash on his temple. A pool of blood stained the polished oak floor and had begun to soak into an expensive Moroccan carpet near his head. Dulcie felt a wave of nausea rise in her throat, and she backed out of the room.

Ten minutes later the police had swarmed into the house. Dulcie sat in a large wicker chair on the front porch overlooking the marshes below. She was shaking badly. Jane Whipple put a blanket over Dulcie's shoulders, poured her a glass of brandy, then poured a large one for herself. "Why?" she said. "He was such a sweet fella! Why?"

Dulcie could not speak. She felt very ill. Holding the brandy with both hands, she took a long drink. It slipped down into her empty stomach like a ball of fire. She took another gulp.

A hand on her shoulder made her jump. The brandy sloshed out of the glass and dripped over her fingers. "Slow down there," a soft voice whispered. He knelt in front of her and took the glass, then gave her his handkerchief. She wiped the sticky liquid from her hands and passed it back. He returned the drink to her, pressing the glass back into her hands so that he could feel them. Ice cold. So, she was not faking her reaction. She was truly in shock from what she had seen.

Dulcie slowly regarded his face. She had seen him before.

"I'm Detective Nicholas Black with the Portland Police Department," he said.

She could only nod in response.

"We met a couple of days ago at the museum. Are you able to answer any questions?"

She opened her mouth to speak, and was surprised to hear her own voice. It was hoarse and sounded dull. "Ask what you need."

"I know this is difficult."

Dulcie nodded again in response.

"How long did you know this man?"

"For about a year. I am the Chief Curator at the museum and he is... was... Chairman of the Board. And the Director."

"Do you know why anyone would want to harm him?"

"No. *Yes!*" She had begun to cry. He handed her his handkerchief again, now stained with brandy. "I'm sorry," she sniffed.

"No, no," he replied. "You've been through a shock."

Her mind was not able to focus. "You have a handkerchief," she said, looking down at it. "Nobody has a handkerchief anymore."

He smiled. "People still need them, they just don't know it."

She snuffled her nose in it. "I can't imagine why anyone would want to hurt him. He was such a nice man." The brandy was helping. Her mind was beginning to clear. "The painting… maybe it was the painting. Yesterday he bought a Winslow Homer in New York for the museum and brought it back with him last night. He said he would call me this morning but he never did. He was planning to meet me at the museum with the painting."

Nick looked beyond Dulcie's shoulder. "Johnson," he said sharply to a man nearby. "We need to search the place for a painting."

Johnson looked at him with disbelief. "The whole place is covered in paintings!" he said.

Detective Black turned to Dulcie. "What did it look like?"

"It was a watercolor of a village in Cuba, but I doubt it would have even been unpacked. It was probably in a wooden box about this big," she held out her arms in front of her. They shook so much that the detective took the brandy glass from her again. "And, maybe eight or ten inches thick."

"Is there a safe in the house that you know of? It could be in there."

"Yes, there's a safe in the study, but I don't think it's big enough to fit the whole box in," she said.

The detective nodded at his partner who hurried back into the house. Turning to Dulcie again, Nick said, "Do you know when Mr. Harriman returned last night?"

"Not exactly. He was flying back from New York. He called me just after the auction. He said that he wouldn't be back until late. I think he said it was a nine o'clock flight."

The detective scribbled down the time.

"Do you know which hotel he was at?"

"The Waldorf."

"We'll make some calls."

"Sir, when did it happen? How did it happen? I saw the gash on his head...."

Nick inwardly cringed when she called him "sir." He hoped he did not look that old. "The coroner won't know until after a full examination, but it looks as though it happened quite early this morning. As to how, well...."

"Yes...," she responded flatly.

"He probably didn't suffer much pain. The one quick blow to the temple would have knocked him out almost instantly."

"That's all I need to know," Dulcie said quickly.

"Could I get your full name, address, and phone number? Then I'll contact whoever you want and get you a ride home."

Dulcie told him the information. As he gave her back the glass of brandy, his hand rested on hers. "It's horrible, but we'll sort it out. Go slowly with this," he nodded toward the glass. "I'll be in touch," he said, then left her to stare at the marshes. She saw nothing and was still staring fifteen minutes later when Dan arrived to collect her.

"Dulcie," he whispered, "you're all right. Let's get you home."

Dulcie's gaze fixed on her brother. Her entire body shuddered and she began to sob hysterically. He knelt beside her and hugged her for several minutes, rocking her slowly back and forth. When he felt her relax, he slowly stood with her and walked them both to his old pickup truck. "I'll come back for the Jeep later," he said. They drove back to her townhouse in silence. Once inside, Dan helped his sister to the couch, told her to lie down, and took off her shoes. He spread a heavy old quilt across her. It was warm and familiar, and made her feel safe. "Try to sleep," he said. "I'll come by later."

℈

The sun cast long, low rays into the room when Dulcie finally woke. She saw a note on the coffee table in front of her.

Dulcie,

Dinner is in the fridge. Good chicken soup. Please eat. New box of English Breakfast tea on the counter. I saw you were out. Call me when you're awake and I'll come over if you want. Everything will be all right. They'll sort it out. Don't worry!

- Dan

Dulcie looked dully around the room. She did not want to think. Tea would be good. She slowly got up, turned on a light and went into the kitchen. She held the kettle under the tap and watched the water flow in. As she put it on the stove she realized that it felt as though she was in a dream. Was this a dream? No, it was a nightmare. She decided to call her brother just to make sure.

"Hi Dan."

"Hi! Did you just wake up?"

"Yes. How long was I asleep?"

"I got you back around one-thirty, so most of the afternoon."

"My neck hurts."

"Are you all right? Do you need company?"

Dulcie paused. "No, my neck just has a cramp. I need to eat something and not think. I can't believe this happened. It's so bizarre. I just talked with him last night." She reached into the cupboard and took out her favorite old, slightly chipped mug.

"The police want to talk with you again," Dan said. "I walked back up there to get your car. I asked them not to disturb you today, but they've got a lot of questions."

"I thought they might. I think the detective gave me his number."

"He gave it to me, too. He asked me to have you call him. Anytime he said, even in the middle of the night. Dulcie, he's on top of this. Will you call him tomorrow?"

"I will. I might even call him this evening. Things are starting to get a little more clear."

"Good. I called your doctor, too. She said that you were probably in a state of mild shock. If you need something from her, she said to call. She wants you to rest and stay calm."

"Ha! Easy for her to say."

"Please try though, Dulcie. All right?"

"Okay. Don't worry. I'll call you if I need to talk or anything."

"Do that. I'll see you soon."

"Thanks, Dan. You're the best brother."

"Yeah, I know."

Dulcie hung up the telephone as the kettle began to whistle. She made the tea slowly and drank it black.

Black. She should call Detective Black soon, while everything was still fresh in her mind. She was beginning to feel angry. Why did this happen? He was such a kind man. Why him, of all people? Could it have been a burglar? Mr. Harriman was simply in the wrong place at the wrong time? She looked at the scrap of paper where the detective had scrawled his telephone number. *'I want some answers,'* she thought angrily and quickly picked up her phone.

"Johnson!" barked a loud voice seconds after she had tapped the number.

"What?" Dulcie replied in confusion.

"Oh! I'm sorry. This is Adam Johnson. You probably want to talk to Black."

"Yes, I do. This is Dulcie Chambers. He asked me to call."

"Hold on…"

Dulcie heard a murmur in the background.

"Ms. Chambers. Thank you for calling." Detective Black breathed a silent sigh of relief. "How are you doing?"

"Better, after some sleep. I'm getting awfully hungry, which I think is a good sign."

"It certainly is. You've had a bad shock. You have to take care of yourself. But, having said that, I need to know if I can come by to ask you some questions? Do you feel up to it?"

"Yes, I do. I've slept for most of the afternoon and I'm very awake now."

"Good. I'll be over in half an hour. Do you like Chinese take-out?"

"Sorry?" Dulcie replied.

"You said that you were hungry, and I haven't had dinner yet, so I thought I'd bring something over."

"Oh, yes! It's a very good idea."

"Great. I'll get something generic. Be there in half an hour."

He could not have known that of all the cuisines in the world, Chinese, and especially chicken fried rice, was her absolute favorite.

Nicholas Black called the Red Dragon Palace, then shuffled his pages of notes together into a file folder. He had already run a background check on Dr. Dulcinea Chambers. It was spotless, as he had expected. People in her position were never mixed up in anything. Nor was he, until he chose police work. Now he was privy to everything low and miserable.

His father had insisted that he go to law school, and had even paid the bills, assuming that Nick would join the Boston firm that his grandfather had begun. Nick humored his father and earned his J.D., but never bothered to sit for the bar. He knew that he would never practice. He needed to get away from Boston, away from the tangled mess that his life had rapidly become. He needed a different sort of life.

The detective work had begun completely by accident. He saw a position open with the Portland Police Department as an officer. Without informing anyone in his family, he applied. On his first day of work a fishing vessel drifted ashore with a full cargo of drugs and no crew. Nick was hooked from that day on. He became known in the force as a thorough investigator with an immense knowledge of the law. His promotion to the coveted level of Detective had been the fastest ever in the history of the department.

From Nick's first day as a detective, the veteran Adam Johnson had been his partner. Nick admired him for his years of experience and optimistic nature. He was also astounded by the volumes of food that Johnson could digest in a single sitting.

Nick shoved the rapidly expanding Harriman file into a bag with his usual items: flashlight, wrench set, hammer, gun. He didn't like to wear the piece when it was not necessary. Grabbing the bag, he left the apartment, stepping out into the cool evening air.

Summer was on its way, and summer in Maine was short but typically worth the wait. Warm days, cool evenings, and a little craziness in the air. His days were busiest in the summer. People did strange things after being cooped up for several months, and it seemed they did even stranger things when it was daylight until nine o'clock at night.

He got into his car and drove to the Red Dragon Palace. They knew him well. Then he continued to Dulcie's townhouse. He felt as though he was on a date. "No, you're on duty," he said out loud. When he pulled up in front of her house, he saw her peek though the curtain on the door, then the front light came on. She opened the door before he even knocked.

"Hi. Let me take that." She hoisted the large bag of food away from him before he could answer. "Come on in."

He followed her inside, looking closely at her townhouse, curious about how she lived. The walls were painted a warm beige, the floors were polished wood, covered here and there with soft rugs. Of course she had artwork hanging everywhere, but it was not what Nicholas Black had expected. He had pegged her as a fan of the Impressionists, but instead he saw Asian pieces, edgy Wyeth portraits, and austere seascapes.

"Do you mind eating it straight from the box? What would you like to drink? I have some bottled water and some red wine," she said.

"Thanks, but I'm on duty still. Could I have a glass of milk if you have any?"

"Of course." She poured his milk, then joined him at the table with her glass of wine. He had noticed the bottle in the kitchen. It was an excellent Bordeaux that he had considered buying himself, although at forty dollars, he had to think twice.

"That's a good year for that Bordeaux," he remarked.

Dulcie looked at him with surprise.

Nick smiled. "You didn't think a cop would know his wines, did you."

"I… well… I'm sorry. Yes, I'm a little surprised! How long have you been interested in them?"

"My father has a pretty extensive cellar. I picked up some things from him, I suppose. The rest I've just learned from lots of reading. I considered getting that Bordeaux when Pat's Cellars stocked it this week. It's a bit out of my price range at the moment, though."

"It's a bit pricey for me too, but wine is my one indulgence," she admitted. "It's a shame you're on duty. I'd be happy to share it with you."

"Thank you," said the detective, feeling himself begin to blush. "Another time."

They were both silent, eating for a moment. She had quite an appetite, he noted. She finished a box of fried rice quickly, then said bluntly, "Why was he killed?"

"I'd like to know that, too. We haven't found anything missing from the house that we're aware of, except the Homer painting. His housekeeper looked through every room with my partner this afternoon, but she didn't notice anything even so much as out of place. At first glance it seems that whoever did it just wanted that painting.

"The airline confirmed that Harriman was on the 9:05 flight from New York. He arrived home a little after eleven last night. His neighbor remembers seeing a car pull in just after her television program had ended. The autopsy indicates that time of death was roughly six o'clock this morning. He hadn't had any breakfast. Do you know if he was normally an early riser?" Nick asked.

"I would say on the average, yes. He often comes by, came by, I should say," she added, correcting herself. She took a large swallow of wine and continued. "He would come by my office at the museum just as I typically arrived at eight-thirty, and was ready to talk business. I always needed another cup of coffee then, just to match his energy level."

"Did he have any enemies?" Nick asked reaching for a box of sweet and sour chicken.

"I don't know, but I can't imagine he could have. He was a good man, in my experience anyway. He personally recruited me for my position as chief curator, and...," she gulped more wine and looked down at the table for a few moments. Taking a deep breath she said, "I am forever in his debt for everything that he did for my career and for the museum. Without him, the state of fine arts in Maine would not be as advanced as it is right now."

"Yes, he did a number of very good things," Nick agreed. He asked Dulcie about her last conversation with Mr. Harriman. Did she recall anything unusual? Did she speak with him while he was in New York, other than to hear that he had successfully bought the painting? Dulcie answered everything as carefully and thoughtfully as possible, stepping painstakingly though the past three days.

Nick sat back at last. Dulcie visibly relaxed as well. She sipped her wine, watching him finish taking notes. He put down his pen and looked up at her. "Just out of curiosity, how and when did you first meet Joshua Harriman? Was it the job interview?"

Dulcie knew what he was getting at. She was young for her position, only twenty-five years old. The obvious assumption was that Dulcie had known Mr. Harriman before coming to the museum, perhaps even years before.

"I know what you're thinking," Dulcie smiled. "But I've only known Joshua Harriman in a professional capacity, not as a family friend or anything. It's kind of an interesting story," she added.

"I'm all ears," Nick replied.

"I was the brainy kid back in high school and actually finished early, when I was sixteen. I still lived at home when I started college – my mother said I was too young to go live in a dorm," Dulcie laughed. "She was probably right. Anyway, I finished my bachelors at age twenty, then had my sights set on graduate school."

"Not *just* grad school. Oxford University," Nick interjected.

"Yes, that," Dulcie answered humbly. She looked at him pointedly. "You've done your homework I see!"

Nick nodded. "Part of the job"

She continued, "I couldn't believe it when I was accepted. And I loved it over there."

"So is that where you met Harriman?" Nick asked.

"No, that didn't happen until later. I'd received my doctorate and was back in the US interviewing for positions with museums. I had some time on my hands and a little money, so I decided to make one last trip before launching into my career. I'd learned Italian at Oxford and had been to Italy briefly, but wanted to go back, so that's where I went.

"The thing is, I don't enjoy flying, so instead of going over the Atlantic in a plane, I decided to see if I could cross on a ship. I found a cruise ship that was ending it's run in the Caribbean and crossing back over to Europe. It wasn't an official cruise, so not many people were on board. They seated us all together at dinner, and I started talking to the older man beside me on the second night."

"And let me guess, that was Joshua Harriman," Nick added.

"Right. I didn't know who he was at the time, but after talking a lot about art, I learned that he was on the board of directors for the Maine Museum of Art. He told me that they were about to initiate a search for a new chief curator. The current one had just announced his retirement. Mr. Harriman said that they wanted someone who understood the 'aura and mystique', as he put it, of the Maine art community through history. He asked if I would be interested in applying for the position. I remember thinking that 'interested' was the understatement of the century.

"The next morning I brought him my CV. He looked impressed and said he needed to make some calls. A couple of days later, he offered me the job. We hadn't even arrived at port yet," she concluded.

"That's pretty amazing!" Nick replied. "I'm surprised he had the authority to make the decision on his own," he said.

"I was too, at the time, but seeing how things operate at the museum, Mr. Harriman is the one who's pretty much in charge." She stopped quickly and looked down at the table. "Well, he was in charge," she corrected herself.

"This is difficult, I know," Nick said.

"Yes, it is," Dulcie admitted. "It isn't that I knew him very well, it's just that I respected who he was and how hard he worked. His fortune was self-made. He was so generous with it, too. It just isn't right…" she trailed off.

Nick pushed back from the table and stood. He began collecting the containers. Dulcie stopped him. "No, no! I'll clean up. It's the least I can do since you brought me dinner. Besides," she smiled sheepishly, "I'm not sure I'm done yet."

Nick laughed as he turned toward the door. "Thanks for the candid conversation. It helps a lot. We'll work with this information for a while. If there's anything else you remember, anything at all, please call me."

"Yes," she replied. "Will you call me if you learn anything?"

"You have my word. Thanks for your help."

"Thanks for the dinner. I owe you one."

"I won't forget." He smiled at her.

Dulcie found herself thinking that his eyes looked like warm, soft gray flannel. She followed him to the door and opened it. "Good luck," she managed to say.

As he walked toward his car, Dulcie heard him whistling softly. Whistling! She jumped through the doorway and ran after him.

"He was whistling!" She exclaimed, grabbing Nick's arm to stop him.

Nick looked at her quizzically. "Does that mean anything? Was it a particular song?"

Dulcie shook her head. "No, not that I could make out. It isn't so much the song, it's the fact that he was whistling. When he left my office on Wednesday, he had just volunteered to go to New York and bid on the painting. He left whistling! He never whistled unless he was nervous about something. He told me that once."

"Wouldn't he be nervous about spending that much money at an auction?"

"No, not him. That was normal for him." She let go of Nick's arm and looked at the sidewalk feeling confused and embarrassed. "I'm being silly now, though. It was only a little whistling, after all. Probably nothing."

"Ms. Chambers, in my business, 'nothings' are usually the biggest 'somethings' of all." He shook her hand. "I'll be in touch."

Dulcie smiled weakly and went back into the house.

*If you could say it in words
there would be no reason to paint.*
— Edward Hopper

CHAPTER 8

Dulcie tried to go to bed, but she lay awake for several hours, partly because she had slept all afternoon, but also because she was trying to remember everything about the room where she had last seen Mr. Harriman. She attempted to keep the image of him lying on the floor out of her thoughts as much as possible, but was not successful. Detective Black had said that Harriman had been killed by a blow to the head with a blunt object. "Sounds like a really bad detective story," she murmured. A blunt object. Were there any blunt objects in the room? Did she notice anything missing? She had been in that room many times before, and now she imagined herself walking through it again. Nothing was clear.

She sighed, exasperated, and threw off the covers. Her glowing green alarm clock read 3:04 AM. "OK, I guess I won't be getting any more sleep tonight," she said to no one. Sliding on her slippers and robe, she went to the kitchen to make a cup of tea. On her way, she grabbed a sketchpad and pencil from her briefcase.

As the water was heating, she slowly began to draw the study at Mr. Harriman's mansion. She drew the walls first, then the paintings on them, which she remembered best. Then she added the furniture. As the pencil moved across the page, details came to her rapidly, and she scribbled them down furiously. Her concentration was so intense that the shrill sound of the teakettle whistle made her gasp before she realized what it was. She stopped and made her tea with a liberal dose of milk in it to settle her nerves.

Dulcie looked carefully at her drawing. Did she remember everything? Probably not. She went into the living room and sat on the couch, curling her legs under her, not taking her eyes off the sketch pad. She sipped her tea slowly. Her eyes blurred and lost focus as she thought about the scene from only the day before. "It was horrible," she whispered. It had been so still and quiet. Not like when you walk into an empty room, but even more quiet. Wouldn't Mr. Harriman have turned his radio on? She knew that he liked to listen to classical music while he worked. Perhaps he had needed to concentrate on something. Perhaps it was too early. Perhaps he had just entered the room.

Fatigue began to sink through her mind. Her head nodded forward, and she snapped it up with a jerk, spilling her tea. *'I can probably get to sleep now,'* she thought wryly and went back to bed.

In the distance, Dulcie heard a doorbell. She turned over. There it was again, louder. She was about to pull up the covers when she realized that it was her doorbell. She sat up quickly. Clear, bright sunlight streamed in between the curtains and onto the soft white down comforter on her bed. She threw off the covers and grabbed her robe.

Dulcie heard loud knocking and her brother's voice. "Dulcie? You okay? You in there?" The sound of a key turning in the lock followed, and she walked down the short flight of stairs to the ground floor just as Dan stepped inside. "Hey, Sis! Sorry to barge in! I was kind of worried since it's noon already and I hadn't heard from you. How are you? Getting enough sleep? Your hair looks great!"

Dulcie swatted him on the arm. "Shut up. Yes, I'm doing fine, but I really need some coffee."

"Coming right up."

"Can you wait for me a few minutes? I want to take a quick shower."

"Coffee will be ready when you come out."

When she emerged from the shower ten minutes later with her hair wrapped in a towel, she felt more refreshed and awake than she had expected. She followed the smell of the coffee and watched while Dan poured her a cup. "Milk?" he asked.

"Always," she replied.

"What's this?" Dan pointed to her sketch from the previous night.

"I woke up in the middle of the night and couldn't get back to sleep. I was trying to remember everything about Mr. Harriman's study. That just started to flow," she said taking the mug that he handed her.

"Is this the way you saw it yesterday, or the way you remember it from before?"

"The way I remember it. I don't think I noticed much of anything yesterday after seeing him…" She took a big gulp of coffee.

"That detective called me this morning. He didn't want to bother you if you were still asleep. They're going to read Harriman's will this afternoon. The attorney said that you should be present."

"Me? Why?"

"Apparently you're mentioned."

"Seriously? Why?" she repeated. "It must have something to do with the museum. Oh no!" Dulcie exclaimed, smacking her forehead with her hand. "Has anyone contacted Alicia? She's been in Boston this week. I think she was coming back on Friday night, but she may have stayed down there over the weekend."

"I'm sure the lawyer tracked her down. They probably called the museum and found out where she was. Don't concern yourself with that."

Suddenly a large grin spread across Dulcie's face.

"What is it?" asked Dan.

"Oh, it's awful, to find pleasant things in the face of tragedy, but I was just wondering if I have to keep Alicia on the payroll anymore? Of course I should, and I will, but I don't have to employ her as a favor to her

Uncle any longer. I do feel bad though, to have such a selfish, nasty thought so soon!"

"Selfish, maybe, but not so nasty, considering Alicia," Dan said, and Dulcie laughed. He looked at the sketch again. "You should show this to the detective," he said. "It could be helpful."

"That's a good idea. I will. I want to look at it for a little while longer, though. I think I've forgotten something."

"What? The blunt object?"

Dulcie frowned, ignoring his black humor. "I don't know. Just something."

"Well," Dan turned to pick up the keys that he had tossed on the counter, "Let me know when you figure it out. Now, do you need a ride to the will reading? It's at three o'clock at Hastings & Wexler, Monument Square."

"Dan, that's only five or six blocks from here."

"I know, but you've been shaken up a little."

"I'll be fine. I could use a good walk."

"All right. Call me if you need anything." He affectionately punched her arm and opened the door.

"I will. Thanks. And, thanks for worrying."

"Anytime. That's my job!" He called over his shoulder.

Dulcie closed the door slowly. She carefully locked it behind him.

At five minutes before three o'clock, Dulcie arrived at the law offices of Hastings & Wexler. She had only attended one will reading before, that of her father. It had been much more informal since the family's attorney was Dulcie's uncle and since the reading was in the living room of her parents' home. Now her heels clicked across the cold marble floor as she followed the office assistant to the conference room of the otherwise empty building. The young man opened the door for Dulcie and said, "I believe everyone else is here." Dulcie hesitated for a moment. Several people were already seated in the room. They all turned toward her at the same time.

"Good, Ms. Chambers! You got my message," said Mary Hastings, Mr. Harriman's attorney. "I'm glad you could come. Now if you could take a seat here, we'll get started."

Dulcie sat next to Ms. Hastings and looked around the table. The only familiar faces were those of Jane Whipple, looking slightly puffy and red under the eyes, Alicia Harriman, looking icy as ever, and James Harriman. *I wonder what I look like to them,* she thought. She sensed someone behind her, and turned to see Detective Black slip into the chair next to her. "You look tired," he said in a low voice.

"I've had plenty of sleep. Just not at the right hours," she whispered. He nodded, understanding. Dulcie continued to look around the table. The few others must be relatives, she thought.

"Mr. Harriman's will is very straightforward," said Ms. Hastings. "It reads as follows:

I, Joshua Harriman, being of sound mind and body, bequeath the following items upon my death:

To my brother, James Harriman, I leave the sum of $250,000 to use as he wishes, as well as lifetime tenancy to my house. Upon his death the house will be sold and the proceeds will go to the Maine Museum of Art.

To my cousins Jack, Gerald, and Jerome, I leave $10,000 each.

To my niece, Alicia, I leave $1,000. Tell her she needs to learn to make her own way.

To my housekeeper Jane Whipple, I leave $250,000 and many thanks for putting up with me.

To Dr. Dulcinea Chambers I leave the sum of one million dollars because she is the daughter I never had. I also leave my entire wine collection and my sailboat to Ms. Chambers.

The remainder of my estate is left to the Maine Museum of Art to do with as they wish under the supervision and final decision of Dr. Dulcinea Chambers.

The room fell silent. Suddenly, at the same moment, Alicia began shrieking, Mrs. Whipple began to cry hysterically, and the three cousins began gesticulating and talking loudly. Dulcie focused on the paper in front of Ms. Hastings. She was aware of Alicia pointing at her wildly. The voices grew dim and distant. She felt Detective Black grab her around the shoulders. The voices drew near to her again, and she looked around. Everything was blurry.

"Water!" Ms. Hastings called to her assistant. A glass of water was put into Dulcie's hand and she drank. She sat up straight again and looked around the room as everything began to clear. Alicia was silent now and glaring at her. "Are you all right?" Ms. Hastings asked Dulcie.

"Yes, perfectly," she said, but felt her voice shake.

Ms. Hastings looked around the room. "I want all of you to know that Mr. Harriman made this will six months ago. He came to me of his own accord, and the contents are quite sound and legal. The family may contest it of course, but I must warn you that you will most likely be wasting your time and money. Mr. Harriman has followed legal precedent in this will and any changes made to it at this point would be extremely unlikely. You will be contacted individually regarding the specifics of your inheritances. Now, I believe Detective Black would like to speak to you. I thank you all for coming." She left the room, closing the heavy wooden door behind her.

Nick stood and took Dulcie's arm, helping her to stand as well. "I suggest that you leave now," he whispered to her. "I'll come by your house this evening if that's all right." He opened the door that Ms. Hastings had just departed through. Dulcie nodded and quickly walked, as steadily as possible, back through the marble corridor.

Detective Black turned to the group of people before him and said, "I have just a few more questions for all of you, if you don't mind. I am still investigating a murder."

"We don't have to answer anything!" snarled Alicia. She shoved her chair away from the table with a loud screech and started for the door.

"True, but let me remind you that everyone in this room could now be a suspect unless they can establish a proper alibi," he replied calmly.

Alicia stopped and spun back around to face him. "And what about the one person *not* in this room? Don't you think she had the best reason of all? She did discover the body! Plus, she was quite *close*, shall we say, to Uncle Joshua!"

"Dr. Chambers has already been questioned and most certainly will be questioned again. Now, I suggest that you sit back down with the others," Nick replied quietly. His eyes betrayed an ominous look. Alicia Harriman closed her mouth firmly and returned to her chair. She crossed her arms and glared at the detective.

"I will need to speak with each of you privately. I will need to know your whereabouts on the night of Friday, May 22 and the early morning hours of Saturday, May 23. Ms. Hastings has kindly provided me with an office, so I will begin with you, Ms. Harriman. Please follow me."

Alicia continued to sit for several seconds, then slowly stood, picked up her purse, and haughtily glided through the door opened by the detective. He gestured toward a chair and she sat. Her crisp white blouse, unbuttoned well down the front, gapped open so that

Nick could see her lace bra. Alicia shifted in her seat, causing the gap to widen. He ignored it. "Ms. Harriman, were you close to your uncle?" he asked.

"Of course!" Her voice now dripped with sweetness. "My father and he were brothers."

"Yes, I realize that, as it is a common definition of the term 'uncle.' Do you have any other aunts or uncles related to Mr. Joshua Harriman?"

"What I *meant* was that they were quite close as brothers," she snapped. "And, no, my father and Uncle Joshua had no other siblings."

"You were close to your uncle?"

Her eyes narrowed. "I've said that, yes."

"Tell me his birthday."

"What?"

"If you were close you certainly would know his birthday. Just tell me the month."

She looked down and shifted in her seat again. The blouse now closed conspicuously. "October, I think," she mumbled.

"You think? Don't you know?" he said quietly.

"Of course I know! Yes, it's in October!" Her voice snapped again.

Nick smiled and leaned toward her. "Wrong," he said softly. "It was two weeks ago. Now, why don't you tell me how close you really were to your uncle."

Alicia looked disgusted. She paused, turned her head away, uncrossed and recrossed her legs, then glared back at the detective. "All right. Have it your way. The truth is, I didn't pay attention to him very much. He was an old man with a lot of money. But then he started to become very interested in art, and

I'm in graduate school at Harvard studying Art History. I decided to cultivate more of a relationship with him. He helped me to get the internship at this little Podunk city museum, but he wouldn't help me get in at the Metropolitan in New York. He knows plenty of people there. He could have gotten me a position there if he wanted to. Bastard! Now he leaves me nothing!" She looked as though she was about to spit.

"One thousand dollars is not exactly nothing, Ms. Harriman."

She simply rolled her eyes.

"What were you doing on the evening of the twenty-second and the morning of the twenty-third?"

"I was in Boston researching a painting for the museum. I do anything to get out of this boring little place."

"Where were you staying?"

"At a hotel."

"Can you give me the name of this hotel?" Nick asked patiently.

"The Marriott. Now is there anything else that you wish to annoy me with?"

Detective Black paused and leaned back in his chair. He clasped his hands behind his head. "Just one last thing. Until we can clear up this matter regarding your uncle, it would be best if you didn't leave this Podunk town."

"That's ridiculous!"

"Be that as it may, you'll be staying in Portland for the time being. You may leave this room now, however." He remained seated comfortably in the chair, arms stretched up with his hands still cradling his head. He had no intention of opening the door for her.

She stood and sneered at him, yanked the door open, and stormed out.

Nick shook his head as the door closed with a decided bang behind her. He clicked the pause button on his cell phone where had had been recording the conversation. It had been in plain sight, and he had turned it on after he and Alicia had entered the room, but he did not think she had been aware of it. He made several notes in his pocket notepad, then stood, breathing deeply. The case was certainly becoming interesting. Johnson would be pleased with that.

He stood now and crossed the room quietly. "Could I have Mr. James Harriman next, please?" Detective Black said, poking his head through the doorway.

James Harriman stood slowly. He carefully made his way around the table. He looked down, avoiding anyone's eyes. As he entered the office to talk with Detective Black an odd, gurgling sound emerged from his throat. He leaned against the closed door behind him and shut his eyes.

Nick watched him closely. He had only seen Joshua Harriman's brother once before at the opening of the Homer exhibit. The man before him looked ten years older than the one he remembered. Harriman opened his eyes, located the empty chair in front of him, reached for it, and slid down.

"Detective," he said in a quiet voice. "I feel sick. This wasn't supposed to happen. I can't believe it did happen. My brother was a good man." Harriman choked back a sob.

"Look, if this is too painful right now, I can talk with you in a day or so."

"No, no. I think that it's important. You'll find out soon enough anyway. I've had some trouble. Financially. My wife, my ex-wife that is, places a great deal of blame and guilt on me for our failed marriage. She demands a great deal and even though legally I owe her nothing, I give in. My daughter takes her side and requires a great deal as well. Josh has helped me on many occasions. He's given me quite a bit of money. I'm sure that's why he left me very little of his relatively, except use of the house. He knows, even in death, that whatever he gives me, they'll get eventually. It's always been like that. Always..." James Harriman trailed off, his head drooping. His eyes wandered across the patterns of the carpet on the floor. Nick waited.

James Harriman added nothing else. The detective cleared his throat and said, "Thank you for sharing that with me. I appreciate how difficult this has been for you, in many ways. I need to ask just some routine questions, that's all. If you're ready?"

Harriman nodded but did not look up.

"Can you tell me where you were on Friday evening and Saturday morning between the hours of ten o'clock at night and seven o'clock the next morning?"

Harriman looked at Nick, dazed. "Friday... Saturday... I was at home."

Nick made a note. "Is there anyone that can vouch for you, sir? To prove that you were there?"

Harriman shook his head. "No. I was alone. I'm nearly always alone."

"Do you know if your brother had any enemies?"

Harriman's head whipped up instantly and his eyes shone like marbles. "Enemies! Who could hate Josh? The man about town! Everyone loved Josh! Oh yes, no one could hate the perfect, wonderful, rich, powerful *Joshua Harriman*!" His sarcasm was overwhelming.

"Can I take it that you know of no one who would wish him harm?" Nick asked quietly.

James Harriman's head dropped again. "Yeah, you can take it like that," he muttered.

Nick watched him for several seconds, but no further outbursts seemed to be forthcoming. He dismissed Harriman with a nod, and he shuffled out of the room. Nick wrote in his notebook: JH – Angry. Sarcastic. Worn clothes. Old shoes. Repentant?

He continued to question everyone. The cousins came next. Detective Black soon learned that each led a more dull life than the one before. Two lived farther Downeast while the third was in Portland. All had wives and families and very little contact with Joshua Harriman except at holidays, weddings, and funerals. They all envied him because of his wealth, but that was normal. Nick exhaled loudly after the third had left, citing, once again as had the others, that he had been in bed with his wife from eleven at night until seven o'clock the next morning for the time in question.

One more to go. Mrs. Whipple. She had at last stopped crying, and Nick joined her in the conference room where he thought she would be more comfortable. Her pink polyester top was stained with tears over her large bosom. The handkerchief clutched in her plump hand was soaked. Nick located a box of tissues and put it on the table in front of her. She smiled meekly.

"Mr. Officer, sir, I just can't believe it. I only worked for him for a year! I'm wicked sorry he's gone, but to think he'd leave a wad 'o cash like that to me, and he nevah once told me! Makes me wish I'd been even nicer to him. I mean, I was nice and all, but sometimes, well, you know, sometimes I sure did envy what he had. I'd slam some things 'round in the kitchen once in a while, you know, but never in front 'o him. I was just wishin' that my lot was different, you know?" She started to tear up again and pulled out a handful of tissues.

"Yes, Mrs. Whipple, I know. This has been hard. You've been very brave. May I ask you a few questions?"

"Of course, de-ah," she sniffled.

"Tell me about your normal routine with Mr. Harriman. What happens each day?"

"Well, I'm his housekeepah, but not the live-in sort. I come 'round every day, 'cept Wednesday and Sunday, to clean, straighten up, and do a little cookin'."

"Did Mr. Harriman himself follow a regular routine?"

"Pretty much, unless he's away. He's away quite a bit, though."

"Yes, he traveled often. Tell me his routine when he was around, though."

"Well, I usually show up between seven o'clock and seven-thirty. 'Cept Saturdays. Saturdays I come at noon and Mr. Harriman gets his own breakfast. My husband, he drops me off most Saturdays so he can keep the caah for errands and such. I let myself in."

"Do you have a key? Is the door usually locked?"

"Yes, it is early, weekdays. I got a key, so I unlock it and let myself in, but I don't lock it behind me. Then I go in the kitchen and start makin' coffee and mixin' up some eggs. He likes two eggs scrambled with a half a tomato grilled for breakfast. And a little toast or English muffin. Saturdays the door is sometimes open, sometimes not, when I get there. Don't matter which to me, I just let myself in and holler so I don't spook him or nuthin'."

Nick nodded and took notes carefully.

"In the early mornin' I hear him up and about in his study. He's always dressed and ready for the day when I see 'im. I bring his breakfast and we talk for a little minute. Just small talk, ya know. Then I tell him where I'll be at for the mornin'. Which rooms I'll be cleanin'. He tells me if he's goin' to be in the house or not, and sometimes he tells me where he's off to, if he's goin' someplace."

"Good."

"Then I don't see him again, generally, 'til lunch if he's 'round. He likes to come inta th' kitchen at lunch and see what's in the fridg'rator. On Saturdays, that's usually when I'll see him first – when he comes inta th' kitchen. Sometimes he'll ask me to get somethin' for him, but sometimes he gets it his-self."

"And after lunch?"

"Aftah lunch he takes a long walk, then comes in, listens to a radio program – some talk show, I think, and news – then I leave 'round four o'clock or so when Whipple comes round to get me."

"Very good, Mrs. Whipple. Only a couple of questions more. Did Mr. Harriman seem bothered by anything, or did he do anything differently on Thursday before he left for New York?"

She thought for a moment. Her mind was working harder than it had in years. "He didn't go for no walk. Just stayed in his study. I looked in on him once and he was just starin' outta th' window. Looked like somethin' was on his mind. He'd just gotten his mail, too, so there was a lettah in his hand."

"Do you believe it was the letter that he was thinking about?"

"Couldn't say, sir. Could be. He gets lotsa mail, lotsa lettahs, from all ovah the world. My grandson, he's eight, and he collects them stamps, so Mr. Harriman gives me the pretty ones for him sometimes."

"Would you be able to identify which letter was in his hand?"

"No! I'm not no snoop, sir! Plus, he gets so many and they all look the same to me. I just like to look at the stamps. For my grandson."

"Yes, I understand. Did you know that he would be mentioning you in his will?"

"Certainly not! My goodness! Whipple and me wanted to get one o' them nice condos on the ocean in one o' them retirement commun-tees. The old house inland is just too big for us. Can't keep up with all them repairs and such nowadays. But we didn't have no spare money, even if we did sell the house 'cause it's wicked rickety now and we don't got much land. We wouldn't get much for it if we sold. But, bless his soul…" She began to cry again.

"That's all right Mrs. Whipple. One last thing. You were with your husband on Friday evening and Saturday morning?"

"Yes, and my sistah, she come over Friday night, too, for suppah. She stayed till 'bout ten o'clock or so, then Jed and me went to bed. Didn't get up till 'bout eight-thirty, I think. I sleep in a little on Saturday mornings, 'cause I can you know. It's my in-dull-gence," she pronounced the word proudly.

"Yes, I know how good it is to get a little extra sleep. Can you tell me anything else that seemed different about last week? Anything that changed in Mr. Harriman's manner?"

"Well, he did have that small tiff with his brother. He's always needin' to get bailed out. Spends too much or sumthin' though you'd never know it to look at him."

Nick sat back and reviewed his notes quickly. "Mrs. Whipple, I think that's all that I need from you for the moment. May I contact you again if I have any more questions?"

She smiled and sat up straight. "Why yes. Of course, de-ah. I'll do what I can to help," she said importantly.

"Thank you. Do you need a ride back home now?"

"That would be awfully kind." She looked at him shyly. "Would it be in a police caah with one o' them blue lights on the top?"

Detective Black smiled. "Yes, I believe it would."

A giggle slipped from Mrs. Whipple's lips.

ଔ

Dulcie slowly walked down Congress Street. It seemed unnaturally quiet on a Sunday afternoon. "What the hell is going on?" she said to no one. "Why would he leave me that kind of money? I can see the museum getting it, but me? Plus, what's this about *the daughter he never had?*" She rounded the corner of a building, stepping onto Exchange Street and nearly ran headlong into Tom Cole. Grabbing his arm for support, she gasped, "Tom! Hi! I thought you were up in Brunswick!"

Tom mumbled something and looked away. "They didn't need my help after all so I came back early," he said more clearly. He stepped back so that Dulcie had to let go of his arm.

"Then I suppose you've heard the news about Mr. Harriman?"

"Uh, yeah. Just heard it at the Dock." Dulcie thought she had detected the faint odor of alcohol. The Dock was a popular waterfront bar.

"It's horrible, isn't it?"

"Yeah. It's pretty bad."

"I'm so angry about it," said Dulcie. "There's no reason why anyone would do that to him."

"You're right. Um, I gotta go. I'll be at work tomorrow. See ya then." He turned and left abruptly.

'*He's in a hurry,*' thought Dulcie. She continued home, ate the leftovers from Detective Black's Chinese food, and went straight to bed.

CHAPTER 9

The funeral was scheduled for eleven o'clock on Monday morning. Dulcie arrived early after stopping at the museum first to check her messages. In the church she saw many familiar faces. Tom was nearest. She smiled at him and sat in a pew near his.

The service was as pleasant as could be expected. Afterward the casket was taken to the cemetery. Most of the people from the church service gathered to see it lowered into the ground, paying their final respects.

Detective Black stood across from Dulcie, slightly behind the remainder of the crowd. He nodded at Dulcie, and she watched him as he intently eyed everyone. Was the person who killed Joshua Harriman standing there with them now? Her eyes scanned the group. Dulcie saw Alicia, looking even more stunning in skin-tight mourning black, but with very dry eyes. The cousins, as dopey as ever, in ill-fitting dark suits. The brother, looking sufficiently distraught. Mrs. Whipple, leaning against her husband with a tissue held to her nose. Then, Dulcie's eyes fell on another woman whom she had never seen before. She looked as though she was ready to faint. Dulcie watched her step back through the crowd. To Dulcie's surprise, Tom stepped back as well, put his arm around the woman, spoke to her in a low voice, and led her away.

The service ended and Dulcie followed the group to the church rectory for coffee and sandwiches. She ate little and gulped down two cups of coffee, her teeth grinding anxious marks into the white Styrofoam. Then she quietly slipped away and went back to her office.

Once inside she closed the door, crossed to the window and threw it open wide. The smell of the rising tide drifted up. She inhaled deeply. She heard a ship sound its horn in the harbor. *'Life goes on, but not for him,'* she thought. She heard a tap at the door and turned from the window. "Come in," she called, not really wanting to face work issues but knowing that she could not escape them.

Detective Black entered and closed the door behind him. "Well, that's that, but my work has only just begun. Do you have a moment?"

Dulcie nodded, relieved that it was him. He had a way of making her feel relaxed. "Let me hang this up," she said as she shrugged off the light cotton jacket that she wore over her dress. She opened the small closet in the corner of her office. Reaching for a hanger, she looked down and gasped. Dulcie jumped back, dropping the hanger and the jacket. Nick was beside her in an instant. He watched her quizzically as she gaped at what appeared to be a small painting lying in the bottom of the closet.

"*That* was not here before!" exclaimed Dulcie. "It's the Homer that Mr. Harriman bought in New York!"

"Are you sure that's the painting he bought?" asked the detective.

"Yes, absolutely!" She stooped down to pick up her jacket and the hanger that had clattered to the floor. "I came in earlier this morning to get my messages. I grabbed this jacket, too. It was in the closet."

"Don't touch anything!" said Nick. He left the office for a moment, and Dulcie heard him on his cell phone. Ten minutes later, a police photographer was snapping pictures of her office. Dulcie was asked to close the museum immediately.

'*The killer was here. In my office,*' she thought. '*What if I had come in while… what if I had surprised him?*' The police were everywhere now, rolling out yellow tape to section off her office, bringing out kits of tools to take fingerprints, and flashing cameras from every angle.

Dulcie sat on one of the padded leather benches in the main gallery watching the activity around her. It did not make any sense. Detective Black approached, looking at her questioningly. She nodded, and he sat beside her.

"I suppose that this makes me a suspect."

"Yes, it does," he replied quietly. "You have been all along. However, unless you spent many years in acting school, I doubt that your reaction to finding the painting could have been dramatized so well, solely for my benefit. Besides, you didn't even know I was coming over."

"True, but I'm still a suspect, and that's fine because if I am, then many others are too, and I want you to rule out no one." Her back stiffened and she quickly turned to face Nick. "Rule out *no one*! Do you hear me? I want to know who did this, and I want to know *now*. It's ludicrous! He was a kind man, and the person who killed him was a monster! Tell me what to do, and I'll help. Say it!"

Nick reached out and took her hand. "Thank you. You've helped a great deal already," he said in a quiet voice. He looked down at his hand holding hers and released it nervously.

Taking a deep breath he said, "What I need now is the complete cooperation of your staff. I'd like to establish a pattern of activity here, to know everyone's comings and goings. I'm sorry to say that very often in cases like these, the killer is someone that everyone knows. He, or she, is harboring a grudge, fear, rage, or jealousy. I need to see the pattern of this place, then determine who doesn't fit, or who broke that pattern."

"I'll make a list of the staff and the volunteers. Would a list of our regular visitors be helpful also? A handful of people are doing some research, and there's a sketch class that meets here each week."

"Perfect. Can you do that right now?"

"Yes, if I can get into my office."

"Let me make sure they're done dusting for prints."

Dulcie suddenly laughed. The sound of it echoed oddly through the empty gallery. "You detectives really say that?"

Nick smirked. "Yes, I'm afraid we do."

A few minutes later Dulcie was at her desk with the personnel files open on her computer. The museum had a regular staff of twenty people, not including Dulcie. The volunteers numbered twelve. She could think of eight regular visitors, including the sketch class. The list included forty-one names. She compiled them, then added the addresses and telephone numbers of each. She printed the list and handed it to Nick.

"You're a wonder," Nick said. "Johnson!" he called out. His partner stuck his head around the corner. "We need to talk to all of these people right away." Nick walked over and handed him the list. "See who has an alibi for the time of the murder, as well as the time between quarter of eleven and noon today. Also, ask everyone when they normally work, and if there were any changes in their scheduled hours last week. Let me know as soon as you're done." Adam Johnson nodded and hurried out the door, calling to another officer as he did.

"All right. Now, tell me when the first staff person usually arrives, who opens the place, who arrives next, etc., etc."

"I'm generally one of the first, but usually when I arrive, I smell coffee, which means someone else is already here. The person drinking the most coffee around here, besides myself, is Alicia. She prefers hazelnut, which is most often what I smell. Then, I hear a couple of other staff members at the main information desk, and Tom usually pops his head in sometime early on.

"Do you get coffee first thing when you come in?"

"No, not right away. I have some at home before I arrive, then I usually don't have another cup until around nine-thirty or ten o'clock. By then we're typically on our second pot."

"The kitchen is near your office?"

"I share this wall with it," she pointed behind her, "but the doorway is off the main information desk. I have to leave my office, walk behind the desk, then go into the kitchen."

"Did you follow this routine last week?"

"For the most part, yes."

"Do you remember if everything during the past week was just as you described it now?"

"Yes, except the coffee was different. Alicia was away last week. I think Tom might have made it. He prefers plain old Colombian, '*Not the stuff the broads drink*,' as he so quaintly puts it."

Nick laughed. He asked, "Is there anyone who no longer works here, that may still have access to the building?"

Dulcie shook her head. "No. There's a pass code that we enter into the security system to access the building when we're closed, or to use the staff entrances. The code changes every time someone leaves our staff. Volunteers are not given the code. We also need to scan our security badges every time we enter, and the system records who is in the building. Our security director can give you the more technical description."

"So, you have security cameras at the entrances?"

"Dulcie nodded. "Yes, but they're not under continuous observation. We don't have enough staff to cover that, but we do record the images from them. There's no sound, just the image."

"Good. I'll talk with security and get the data files that we need." Nick looked down at his notes. "So, Alicia Harriman was away last week?"

"Yes, she was doing some research in Boston on a lesser-known artist."

"Were any other staff members out during the week?"

Dulcie thought for a moment. "Tom asked to leave early on Friday, to help out his family in Brunswick. His dad and brothers are all lobstermen. Tom and I met on Friday morning in my office, but I told him that he could leave after that." She looked beyond Nick for a moment, thinking. "It's odd, because I thought I saw him on Saturday around noon, on my way over to Mr. Harriman's…" she stopped, squinting her eyes as if to think better, "but, I don't think that it really was him. It was only for a few seconds."

"Did anyone else request Friday or Saturday off?"

"None of the regular staff, but most of the volunteers only work for a few hours per week, and when they can't come, they report to their supervisor rather than me. I can get you a schedule of their hours if you like, but you'll need to talk with the volunteer director to find out if any of them switched hours."

"I'll do that."

"The only person that I'm aware of who was away all day on Friday was Alicia Harriman. She called me on Thursday afternoon and said that she needed to spend another day in Boston. I don't know if she came back to Portland on Friday night, or if it was sometime during the weekend."

"I'll check. Tell me," he stopped and took a quick breath, looking away with some embarrassment. "Did you have any idea of the contents of Joshua Harriman's will?" He hoped it didn't sound like an accusation.

Dulcie knew he had to ask the question. She shook her head. "Honestly, I did not. I was very surprised, especially by the statement that I was, 'the daughter he never had.' It does make me a bit uncomfortable to have received so much when his family got so little in comparison."

Nick nodded, relieved by her answer. "Do you think that Alicia Harriman had any idea?"

Dulcie had to laugh. "No! She was more angry than I've ever seen her. And believe me, I've seen her quite angry. I am sure that she thought she'd be getting a large chunk of his estate."

Detective Black looked out the window thoughtfully. "That'd be quite a motive for anything."

"Yes, sir, it would."

Nick winced inwardly at her formal address. *'Come on, now,'* he thought. *'This is a murder investigation, after all.'* He stood quickly. "I've got to go find my partner and follow up on these inquiries. The painting will be taken to the station as evidence. We'll lock it up well."

"Thanks," said Dulcie. "I'll notify James Harriman to make sure the insurance company knows that it's back, and to see that it's insured while it's on 'temporary loan' to you." She grimaced. Detective Black nodded and left the room.

Dulcie sat at her desk for several moments. Her thoughts raced, but soon began to slow and form distinct groupings. She let her mind continue in this manner until it had rested on the painting again. Something concerned her about it. What was it? It seemed odd that anyone, even a murderer, would leave it lying around, given its value. It also seemed odd that they would give it up in the first place. Were they trying to implicate her? Perhaps the motive to kill Mr. Harriman wasn't to steal the painting? She needed to know more about it.

Dulcie decided to call her contact at the auctioneers. He could have more information on previous owners, or he might know something unusual that could help her. She looked up a number on her cell phone and pressed the call button. "Hello? Dr. Dechamp? This is Dulcie Chambers at the Maine Museum of Art….Yes, we just purchased the Homer… um, yes, I have seen it, sort of, but I was wondering if there was anything unusual about it, or the sale? Yes… What? What copy? …Two? …Yes, I understand. Thank you! Goodbye!" Dulcie hand shook as she put down the phone.

ᘓ

Dulcie and Detective Black sat in an office at the police station. "Tell me again?" he asked.

"I think that we should have the painting analyzed. I just spoke with Christie's, and they told me that there were two paintings: the original and a copy. Apparently the previous owners needed the money from the sale, but didn't want to part entirely with the painting. They had a copy made for themselves, but then they couldn't bear to look at the copy knowing that it wasn't the original work, so they included it in the sale with the original. If the painting that we found in my office isn't the real one, I think that we can narrow our field of suspects considerably to those who would know which painting was which, and those who would be willing and able to sell a pretty major painting on the black market."

Nick sat back in his chair and blew out a long, low whistle. "Wow," he said. Then he looked intently at Dulcie. "Would you know if it was a copy?"

"Thank you for the compliment, but beyond a visual examination, I wouldn't be able to tell, unless it had been done rather sloppily. My initial glimpse of it in the closet at my office was quite convincing. I think we probably need an expert to analyze it."

"Would you look at it anyway?" he asked.

"Of course," she replied.

Nick led Dulcie to the evidence room. They walked between shelves containing a vast array of items from firearms to clothing to plastic bags of powdered substances. They stopped in front of a door set into a concrete wall. Nick unlocked it and switched on the light.

Dulcie saw the painting, encased in a plastic bag, standing on a shelf at the back of the room. "This is our highest security area," said the detective. He put on a pair of latex gloves, handing a pair to Dulcie as well.

He walked over to the painting and carefully picked it up, took it out of the bag, then held it in front of him so that it faced her.

Dulcie leaned down and scrutinized it intently. "It's very good, if it is a copy. They have his brush technique down, definitely. I really can't say." She straightened up and stepped back. "No, I really don't know. But, I know who would."

"Good. Could you get them here quickly?" Nick questioned.

"I can certainly ask," Dulcie said.

Three hours later a highly paid art expert sporting an expensive linen suit and too much pomade on his thinning hair was sitting in the evidence room, hovering over the painting with a magnifying glass. "Yesssh, yesssh…" He kept repeating. He had just finished a series of tests using various lights and pieces of odd-looking equipment, most of which the detective had never seen, and with which Dulcie was only vaguely familiar. She and Nick looked at each other. Dulcie shrugged her shoulders. Nick looked frustrated. He couldn't wait any longer. "Is it the genuine article, sir?" he asked.

The expert slowly put down his magnifying glass and even more slowly turned to face Nick. Eyeing him as one would look at a bug on a wall he said, "No. It is not a *genuine article*. It is a copy. Furthermore, I believe I can tell you who made it, or I can certainly narrow it to at least two artists."

Nick smiled. "Thank you, sir. Thank you, very much."

"You won't thank me when you get my bill," he replied. Using an expensive fountain pen, he scrawled two names on a piece of notepaper embossed with his initials and handed it to Nick. Then he clicked the case of his magnifying glass closed, packed it and his other equipment into a buttery leather briefcase, and left without uttering another word.

Dulcie tried not to laugh, but wasn't successful.

Nick just shook his head and smiled. "The people I get to meet with this job…!" he said. He handed the paper with the names to Dulcie. "Ever heard of them?"

"No, not at all. They're probably in New York, but they must be well known for their work. Perhaps operating at times on the seamier side of the industry?"

"We've got enough seaminess around already. I'll check them out and let you know what I learn."

"Thanks. Oh, I nearly forgot!" Dulcie reached into her own briefcase and pulled out a sketchpad. "In the middle of the night on Saturday I made this sketch. I couldn't sleep, so I got up and was trying to remember everything that I could about Mr. Harriman's study. I've got a pretty good eye for detail. It comes in handy in my line of work."

"Mine too," said Nick as he took the sketch. "Is this the way you saw it that morning or the way you remember it?"

"Funny. My brother asked me the same question. It's the way I remember it. I don't remember seeing anything that morning after I saw Mr. Harriman." She looked at the floor and spoke more softly, "It was really awful."

Nick watched her for a moment, and then said, "I think that this will help a great deal. I'll compare it with the pictures taken that morning. Maybe something will jump out at us."

"I hope so," Dulcie replied. "I'm going to go home now for supper, unless you'd like to grab a bite somewhere with me now?"

Nick looked away. *'Don't be silly,'* he thought. *'She's not asking you out, she's just being polite.'* He looked back at her and said, "Thanks, but I'm still on duty. I need to finish up some things here."

"All right, but don't forget that I still owe you dinner. I'll talk with you soon."

૯ૐ

Nick remained at the police station until late that evening. He reviewed the evidence painstakingly and tried to keep an open mind. He had learned that if an opinion, even a guess at a solution, was made too early, it would lead his mind astray making him blind to the truth. He made a list of the people without strong alibis, then added their possible motives:

<u>Jane Whipple</u> – Money, if she knew about the will, or if she knew how to sell a Homer on the black market.

James Harriman – Money, from the will or from the painting.

Tom Cole – Money, if he knew how to access the black market.

Alicia Harriman – Money, if she believed she was getting a bigger inheritance or if she sold the Homer. Revenge, since Harriman didn't help her secure a work position at a larger museum.

Dulcie Chambers – Money, if she knew about the will. Or if she sold the painting. Or both.

Dan Chambers – Money from his sister's inheritance, if he knew about it, or from selling the painting.

Unknown burglar – Money, or perhaps a personal grudge against Joshua Harriman.

It seemed that money was right at the top of everyone's list. He made a mental note to double-check the credit records and bank accounts of the suspects. Looking at the list again, he thought, *'I don't like Dulcie's name there. I'm sure she couldn't have done it. I need to get her off this list.'*

Pulling out the file of photographs from the murder scene, Nick went through them until he found one taken of the study from roughly the same angle as Dulcie's sketch. *'I'm looking for differences,'* he reminded himself. He looked back and forth, back and forth, from one to the other. His head moved as though he was watching a tennis match. *Nothing. Nothing. Nothing… Wait!* It was a small table by the window, behind Harriman's desk. In the photograph the table was clear of any objects, but in Dulcie's sketch it looked like she had placed a vertical squiggle on it. It could have been a slip of the pencil, but it might not have been. He looked at his watch. Ten-thirty. Too late to call? No, he thought, she'll probably still be up. He quickly tapped in her number.

"Hello?" Dulcie answered after one ring.

"Hi, Dulcie, it's Nick. Detective Black. I'm sorry to call at this hour, but I need to ask about the sketch."

"I'm still awake. I was just reading. What is it?"

"On your sketch you show a small table near the window behind Harriman's desk. There's a kind of squiggle on the table."

The phone line was silent.

"Are you there?" Nick asked.

"Yes. I'm sorry, I was thinking. Yes, he had a little statuette on it. Stone. A Yucatán pre-Columbian figurine. I think it was a fertility goddess."

"How little?"

"Well, maybe a foot tall, but no more."

Detective Black's heart began to pound. "Thank you."

"Is that all? Was that the right answer?" Dulcie asked.

"Yes, it certainly was. I'll talk with you tomorrow. Good night!" The phone clicked off.

Dulcie sat on her couch thinking about the conversation. *'Maybe that was the murder weapon? It can't be!'* she thought. *'Could it?'*

What Dulcie did not know was that instead of a pre-Columbian fertility goddess, the police had located a long, bleached-blond hair on the same table in Mr. Harriman's study.

CHAPTER 10

Tuesday morning was foggy and dark. Storm clouds had rolled in overnight surrounding the small city and blanketing the ocean. Dulcie heard a foghorn in the distance and threw off the covers. She glanced at the clock and groaned.

An hour later she sat at her desk, staring out of the window into the fog. A tap at the door made her look up. Tom stood in the doorway. "Can I come in?" he asked.

Dulcie motioned to the chair in front of her desk. Tom walked across the room, and Dulcie noticed that his shirt was untucked in the back already. He slouched in the chair, looking tired. "What can I do for you?" Dulcie said.

"Um, I know I asked this before, but I need a little time off again. It's my Mom this time. Dad's healthy enough to be back on the boat, and Mom is at home all alone. Seems this murder has her spooked. She's nervous about me working in a place where a murderer could be running amuck. Those were her words, not mine. I told her not to worry about it, but she is anyway. I think a couple of days with her would set her mind at ease again."

Dulcie sighed. "Under the circumstances, Tom, and we do have very unusual circumstances, I will say yes, take a couple of days off. I'd like to see you again by Friday, though, if that works for you?"

"I'm sure it will. Thank you." He began to leave her office.

"Tom?" Dulcie called to him. "What about the investigation? I was told to stay in town for a few days, until further notice."

"Yeah, I'm going to call that detective and let him know where to find me."

"Good idea. See you on Friday."

After a quick thank-you, Tom silently departed. Dulcie peered at the door after he had closed it behind him. '*Something has him spooked, too,*' she thought, '*and he's not alone. We're all on edge these days.*' She worked quietly in her office for the remainder of the morning until the telephone rang just before noon.

"Dulcie, it's Alicia," she sounded like someone pretending to be upset. "I won't be in at all this week. I can't believe that any of this has happened! Poor Uncle

Joshua! He was my favorite, and…," she broke off for a moment and sniffed loudly.

"That's fine, Alicia. I understand," Dulcie interrupted before Alicia could go on with any more fake sadness. "Take your time and rest. It's a terrible shock, I know. However, I do need that background file on the Homer painting. Could I stop by and pick it up this afternoon? Around two o'clock?"

Alicia hesitated. "Yes, I guess that would be all right. I'll have it ready."

"Thanks. See you then. Take it easy, all right?"

"I will. Goodbye."

Dulcie clicked the phone off. *'Sure he was your favorite,'* she thought, *'but apparently, you weren't his!'* She stuck out her tongue at the phone.

The afternoon sun was making a feeble attempt at shining through the remaining clouds and fog as Dulcie walked to Alicia's waterfront apartment. The view across the bay looked misty and ethereal. *'Only the best for the princess,'* Dulcie thought. She tapped on the door and Alicia answered. Her hair was tousled in a perfect way and her make-up was subtle, to play up a look of weariness, Dulcie noted. It did not fool her, but Dulcie was sure that Alicia's act did fool many.

Alicia seemed genuinely nervous to have Dulcie there, however. She met her at the doorway with the file, handing it to her quickly. She was about to speak when the telephone rang. Looking flustered, Alicia stepped back, opening the door for Dulcie to enter.

Alicia hurriedly answered the telephone and went into the next room, speaking sharply and quietly. Dulcie looked around her. She had only been in Alicia's apartment once before. It was tastefully and sparsely decorated in a very modernist way. The bedroom was immediately to her right and appeared to have a glorious view of the bay. Dulcie stepped into the doorway.

The atmosphere was a bit more lush here. A risqué, for its time, poster of a Toulouse-Lautrec can-can dancer hung over the bed, while a Matisse blue nude decorated the opposite wall. The bedside table also contained several *objets d'art* that looked interesting. Hearing Alicia's footsteps, Dulcie quickly stepped back into the entranceway.

"I'm so sorry. Here's the file that you wanted. I managed to find some good material at the Museum of Fine Arts in Boston. I hope it's helpful."

"Thank you. I'm sure it will be. Is there anything that I can do for you?"

"No, thanks. Mummy is flying in tonight, and we'll sort everything out. Thanks for stopping by." She nearly pushed Dulcie out of the door.

'Hmm,' thought Dulcie, 'anxious to see me go? '

Alicia had never liked Dulcie, which did not bother her in the least. Alicia was the sort of person who felt that the world owed her something simply because she was alive. Her looks and her money had provided her with everything that she could want when she was younger, but the former were definitely showing signs of fading. As for the latter, Dulcie suspected that the trust funds were fading even faster.

Dulcie felt sorry for her at times, but could not bring herself to like Alicia. She had given her an internship at the museum only to honor Mr. Harriman's wishes. Alicia certainly had the credentials to do the job – she was a very intelligent woman with a great deal of knowledge about art – but her personality was so abrasive that Dulcie would never have considered her if Alicia had not been otherwise connected with the museum.

Dulcie walked through the gray streets and back to her office. She got a cup of coffee, then sat back down at her desk. She opened the file that Alicia had given her, but her eyes did not seem to want to focus for longer the two or three minutes at a time. She walked over to the window and watched fingers of fog weave across the bay. The islands were barely visible, only ghostly outlines in the distance. On clear days they looked as if they were so close that she could touch them. Today they seemed to be a thousand miles away.

Maine, she had thought, was such a safe place. People looked out for one another but never interfered. Everyone seemed open and honest, almost to a fault, unless one was a stranger. People 'from away' were not distrusted, they were simply unknown. Until they stayed long enough to become known, which could sometimes take generations, Mainers would deal with them from a polite, safe distance.

Now, however, someone had invaded that safety, perhaps someone that she knew and trusted. Should she be nervous? She was a little, she had to admit, but not really frightened. How could she be any kind of a threat to the killer? She had no information that could lead to him, and she certainly had nothing that he could want. Of course, there was the matter of the million dollars from the will, but Dulcie believed that she would never see that money. She was sure that the will would be contested, and that the money would either be awarded elsewhere or would pay for lawyers' fees. No, nobody would be interested in snuffing out her.

Dulcie saw the nearest island momentarily disappear, then reappear dimly. It would be dark early with all of this thick fog. The view reminded her of Alicia's bedroom view. She laughed softly, wondering what Alicia would think, had she known Dulcie was snooping around her home. *'I wasn't really snooping, though,'* thought Dulcie, *'I was just curious. All I did was step in the door.'* She thought about the sparse decoration. Her mind pictured the bedroom like the islands in the fog, images of things fading in and out. Then, she stared without seeing, her mouth slowly gaping open in astonishment.

She hurried to the telephone and quickly made a call. Detective Black answered. "I've got to talk with you. It's important, but I can't here. Can you meet me at my house after work? …Six-thirty? …Yes. Thank you!" Her heart pounded as she sat at her desk again. She pulled out a sketchpad and began drawing as fast as she could with dark, slashing strokes. Could it be?

Time passed quickly with her mind racing. At quarter past six she turned out her light and left the office. She did not bring her briefcase with her. *'I'll never get anything done tonight,'* she thought. The museum closed early on Tuesdays and was dark as she walked through. She closed and locked the side entrance door, setting the alarm code as she did. The fog had become a heavy mist surrounding her and blocking all but the nearest objects from view. It seemed to soak into her skin. Dulcie wished that she had worn a jacket that morning.

As she quickly walked down the street, Dulcie heard footsteps behind her. *'Glad I'm not the only one working late,'* she thought. She turned a corner. The streetlight overhead had burned out, making the foggy street very dark. She stumbled once, then heard the scrape of a shoe on pavement again behind her. She quickened her pace, but sensed the other person doing the same. The street was growing darker as she continued farther along. *'I must be crazy. There's no one following me,'* she thought. But, just to make sure, she turned and looked over her shoulder. A dark figure loomed behind her and took several steps quickly toward her, closing the gap between them.

Dulcie spun back around and ran, as fast as she could. Her heart throbbed in her throat as a vice-like grip grabbed her arm from behind. She screamed and wrenched free, nearly falling on the rough cobblestones, then caught her balance and ran down an alleyway. She heard running footsteps behind her and darted between two buildings, not paying attention to where she was going. Running as fast as she could, she quickly realized that she had made a wrong turn. She was tearing down a long wharf and she could see the end of it ahead. She had no escape. The tide was out and the wharf stood at least fifteen feet above the water level.

Dulcie screamed again as she felt two hands grabbing her, one of them closing around her neck. She felt a horrible smelling cloth being smeared across her cheek, over her mouth. She twisted hard, breaking free, and, without thinking, jumped into the cold water.

Everything was black. She had never been in such darkness before. The cold shocked her body so that she nearly gasped. She repeated over and over in her mind, *Hold your breath! Hold your breath!* Dulcie had no idea what was around her. She swam under the water for as long as she could until her hand felt a large, hard object in front of her. '*Boat hull,*' she thought. Her hand slid along its shape as she rose through the water, at last reaching the surface.

Her lungs were bursting. She tried not to gasp for air, taking long, silent breaths. Moving slowly, she looked around her. About thirty feet away she saw the wharf and a lone figure dressed in black peering out into the water. Dulcie froze, motionless, then slowly sank below the surface again.

When at last she could no longer hold her breath she rose, gently emerging to the surface. The figure on the wharf was gone, but Dulcie was terrified that he was not far away. She looked around and began to realize where she was. The wharf that she dove from was old and soon to be torn down. It was no longer used for docking boats. The boat that she had found was tied to the next wharf over. She thought she heard a noise on it above her. '*He could be anywhere!*' she thought.

The ocean water was incredibly cold and her fingers began to feel numb. '*I've got to swim toward Durwood's.*

More people will be there,' she thought. Dulcie silently plowed through the water with a modified breaststroke for what felt like miles. She could not tell where she was from underneath the wharves, but knew she must have passed at least three of them. When she reached the next, she swam around the boats docked there until at last she found a rickety looking ladder that reached to the top. She was shivering uncontrollably now, and looked up at the fifteen feet of distance that she would have to climb. "Come on! You can make it," she whispered through chattering teeth. Rubbing her hands together briskly, and not feeling her fingers, she slowly eased her way up the ladder. Her numb fingers could grip nothing, so she hooked her elbows through the slats to hold on. The rough wood bit into her cold, wet skin. When she at last reached the top of the wharf, she huddled with her knees against her chest, overcome with shock and fear.

No one was around. She knew that her cell phone was in her pocket, but it would be useless. As the fog swirled around her, she thought that she could make out an old-fashioned pay phone at the far end of the wharf, closest to land. She tried to stand, but her legs wouldn't hold her. Crawling slowly along the heavy wooden planks, she finally reached the phone. She rose up on her knees with as much strength as she could find and dialed 911, hoping that the phone would actually still work. Then she collapsed with the receiver swinging over her head.

ℭ

Dulcie heard a faint chirping sound in the distance. She felt groggy. She slowly opened her eyes and saw both her brother and Detective Black staring down at her. She blinked.

"Nice hair!" Dan said. "You smell great, too."

"Shut up," Dulcie murmured and smiled. She looked at Nick and said, "You found me."

"Yes, thanks to your call. You managed to locate one of the very few pay phones left in the city. Good work." Nick attempted to sound nonchalant. He tried not to betray his concern as to what could have happened.

A nurse walked over and checked Dulcie's pulse. "You've suffered from mild hypothermia and shock. We have you warm and dry now, though. How do you feel?"

Dulcie closed her eyes for several seconds, and then opened them again. "Tired. And thirsty."

The nurse gave her some water through a straw. Dulcie smiled her thanks. She looked around the room. "When did you find me? How long have I been here?"

"The paramedics picked you up within ten minutes of your call," Nick said. "It's about eleven o'clock now, so you've been in the hospital for at least four hours. Dulcie, if you're feeling up to it, can you tell me what happened?"

"Oh, she just likes to have a swim after work," Dan teased. Dulcie knew from his joking that he was worried.

Nick laughed quietly, but said nothing.

"I was walking home to meet you," she said to him slowly. "It was getting dark, especially because of the fog, and I had a creepy feeling that someone was following me. Apparently, I was right. He tried to grab me, but I ran. I lost track of where I was going and ended up at the end of that old wharf that the city is going to tear down. Whoever it was behind me grabbed me again and tried to shove a horrible smelling rag over my mouth, but I wrenched away and just jumped into the water."

"Damn! Dulcie, I can't believe you had to...," Dan interjected.

"There was nowhere else to go," Dulcie said. "It was so dark and cold in the water. When I came up for air, I could still see him there. So, I sank underwater again. When I surfaced the next time, he was gone. I was terrified he'd still be around, though, so I just swam until I was as far away as I could manage. I don't know how long I was in the water, but it felt like a really long time. Then, I found a ladder on one of the wharfs, climbed to the top, and when I saw a phone, called for help. I don't remember anything after that."

Detective Black and Dan exchanged worried glances. "Do you remember what this person looked like?" Nick asked.

Dulcie was silent for a moment. "No. He was in black, not very big, and didn't seem terribly strong, either. I think that's how I managed to get away."

Nick nodded. "What was it that you wanted to tell me? Why did you want to meet me?"

Dulcie thought hard. Her mind was slowly becoming clear. "Yes! That! I didn't want to say anything at the museum, because I was afraid that someone would overhear. I'm getting paranoid these days."

"Rightly so," quipped Dan.

Dulcie continued, "I was at Alicia's apartment this afternoon to pick up a file. She left me alone when she answered the telephone. I'd only been to her place once before, and I was curious, so I started looking around a little. You'll never believe what I saw! It was that fertility goddess statue! The one that was in Mr. Harriman's study!"

"Are you absolutely sure it was the same one?"

"Yes, as sure as I can be under the circumstances. It's very unusual. Mr. Harriman bought it in Mexico. It's pretty valuable."

"Where exactly was it?" Nick asked.

"On her bedside table. I didn't realize what it was until I thought about it later. That's when I called you," she said to Nick.

Nick had been leaning against the end of the bed. He straightened suddenly. "I have to go. Thank you, Dulcie." He turned to Dan. "Please take care of her?"

"You can count on it," Dan said.

When the detective had gone, Dan turned to Dulcie. "What's going on? What's this all about?"

Dulcie sighed. She was very tired. "Dan, I'm not sure, but I think the statue is the murder weapon. It was in Mr. Harriman's study before he was killed.

Remember the sketch that I made of the study? Nick asked me about it. Actually, he asked me what had been on a certain table in the study after he looked at the sketch. It was the statue, and I just saw it again at Alicia's apartment this afternoon."

"Do you think that she could have…?"

"She'll do almost anything for money, I think."

"Dulcie, listen. Are you sure that it was a man chasing you tonight?"

Dulcie's eyes grew very wide. "No," she said slowly. "I'm not sure."

⚃

Detective Black felt uneasy. He knew where all of the signs pointed, but something bothered him. Was it too simple? No. No murder investigation was ever simple.

He had to act quickly. The attempt on Dulcie's life may have been just that, or it may have simply been a scare tactic. *'She's a very lucky lady,'* he thought. Lucky to be a strong swimmer. Lucky to be quick witted. Lucky.

Was it really luck? Would anyone go to those lengths to secure a million dollars? Deep in his soul he knew that some people would. "Rule out no one," he said aloud. Not even that brother of Dulcie's who seemed to be the salt of the earth. If Dan Chambers knew that Dulcie would inherit, he might have gone to great lengths to make sure that it would happen.

However, in this case all of the evidence seemed to point in another direction. The hair found at the crime scene. The missing statue that Dulcie believed she saw. The assumption of a large inheritance.

He needed to do a search. The wound on Harriman's head was mostly a large bash but did contain a long, linear, deeper gash. If the statue had a heavy rim around the base that matched the wound, he just may have located the murder weapon. Then he would know which suspect he needed to arrest.

The missing painting bothered him. The business of the statue seemed far too simple. Detective Black believed that the answer to the entire case would be with the painting. "Find the painting, and you've found the murderer," he said. The rest would fall into place.

He went back to the police station and filled in the necessary paperwork for the search warrant. *'Better get at this right away,'* he thought. No sense in giving her time to hide the thing, or dispose of it. He made arrangements for the search, then called his partner.

"Yeah?" a groggy voice on the end of the line answered.

"Who said you could sleep? We've got a murder to think about."

"Hey, I'm an old man now. Can't keep up with you young fellas without my Zs. Wha'd'ya need?"

"Well, how about doing a search in about six hours?" Nick asked.

Johnson suddenly became more alert. "What have you got?"

"Dulcie's awake now. She's okay. She wanted to meet with me earlier this evening because she thinks she spotted that little statue that was missing from Harriman's study. You'll never guess where."

"Enlighten me."

"In Alicia Harriman's bedroom."

"Whew!" exclaimed Johnson. "Is she sure?"

"She's got a good eye for those things. She's as sure as she can be, given that she didn't have long to see it without the little witch around."

"Do you think it's what clocked the old guy, too?"

"I'm sure gonna get it tested for everything! Blood, hair, anything they can come up with. I just requested the search warrant."

"Good. Now you go get some sleep. When should I meet you?"

"Six in the morning, at her apartment. I've got it under surveillance right now in case she tries to skip out with the evidence."

"Great. Good work. All right, I'll see you in a few hours." Nick heard him stifle a yawn.

"Thanks. G'night Johnson." Nick turned out the light on his desk and went home, knowing that he would crawl into bed, but get little sleep.

☙

Dulcie lay awake in the hospital, staring at the ceiling. The other bed in her semi-private room was officially empty, so Dan had commandeered it half an hour before. He lay there breathing heavily, and Dulcie knew he was asleep. She looked up at the IV bottle in the dim light and watched the clear fluid drip down.

Nothing made sense. Alicia was selfish, vain, and sometimes even cruel, but never did Dulcie think that she would resort to murder. Especially not twice. Dulcie tried to recall, with all of the clarity that she could muster, the events over the past several days. She knew that she must have the key to it, somehow. Why else would she be a threat to anyone? Reaching over, Dulcie pressed the button to raise her bed up to a sitting position. The humming noise woke Dan instantly.

"You okay?"

"Yes. I'm just thinking. Or trying to. Dan, could you do me a favor and see if you can find a cup of tea in this place?"

He swung his legs over the edge of the bed. "I'll go ask the nurse." He looked back at her and smiled. "Don't go anywhere!"

Five minutes later he returned with tea for both of them in mismatched mugs. "The cafeteria was closed, but they took pity on me at the nurses' station and boiled some water. Pretty nice folks."

"Most people are," Dulcie said as she reached up for one of the mugs. "Dan, I need to think this through out loud. Are you awake enough?"

"I am now."

"Sorry. Really, though, I need to go through this from the beginning."

Dan nodded and sat down on the foot of her bed.

Dulcie took a tentative sip of her tea, then blew on the top. She looked up at her brother. "On Thursday,

Mr. Harriman volunteered to fly down to New York so that he could bid on the painting."

"Who knew about that?" Dan interrupted.

"Everyone at the museum, I expect. We were all buzzing about it. The purchase in general, I mean."

"So he flew down there, but when exactly?" asked Dan.

"He flew down on Thursday night. It was the night before the auction. He called me from his taxi when he had arrived in New York, but I heard nothing else from him until late in the afternoon on Friday, when he called to tell me that he had the painting."

"Did anyone else know about that?"

"No one that I know of. I didn't tell anyone."

"What happened that day? Ordinary stuff?" asked Dan.

"More or less. Alicia was supposed to be back, but she'd called from Boston on Thursday afternoon and said she needed another day for the research. Tom left early on Friday morning to help out his family on the lobster boat. He said that his Dad had the flu."

"You were okay with him taking the time off?"

"Of course. He was just finishing up a project for me, so we talked about it, and then I gave him the rest of the day off."

"Was this before or after Harriman called?"

"Before."

"So he could have been there still when you got the call about the painting?"

"Yes. Yes, he could have, but he seemed anxious to leave."

"How easy is it to pick up the phone at the museum on more than one extension?" Dan asked.

Dulcie thought for a moment. Usually she talked with Joshua Harriman on her cell phone since they often spoke at hours when she was not in the office. Suddenly, she remembered that this call had been different. He had not called her cell phone.

"Dan! Mr. Harriman called on the main museum number! He didn't call me on my cell like he usually does! I answered because I knew that no one was on the front desk right then, but anyone else could have picked up an extension and listened in! Anyone in the museum at the time, who had access to a phone, could have known that Mr. Harriman would be coming home that night with an incredibly expensive work of art with him!"

"So who was there in the museum with you?" Dan asked.

"I wish I knew," Dulcie answered. "I think we should let Detective Black know all of this." She wondered if she should call Nick right away, but decided to wait until she had thought through everything.

"Let's keep going," Dulcie said. "I went home as usual on Friday night after I'd talked to Mr. Harriman. He said that he would arrive back in Portland late and would call me first thing on Saturday morning. We were going to meet at the museum. I waited and waited for him to call, but he never did, so at noon I went over to his house. The housekeeper was already there, but she seemed to be acting in a normal way, although I did overhear the end of a strange phone conversation she had. Something about gambling. She told me that she thought Mr. Harriman had gone out for a walk because the door was unlocked when she had arrived. She hadn't heard him around in the house. I thought it was strange he would go out and leave the door unlocked with a very expensive painting lying around, so I went in the study to look for it."

"Yes, and I know the rest," said Dan.

"After the scene in Mr. Harriman's house, you brought me home, and I slept."

"The next day, Sunday, did anything happen then?"

"No, that's when the Detective…"

"Who happens to be sweet on you," Dan interjected.

"Oh, stop it! He is not! He's just being kind because I've been through a lot. Getting back to the point," Dulcie glared at her brother for a moment, "Sunday was when they read the will. It was, I suppose, your typical will reading with petty, hysterical family and friends," she said sarcastically.

"And I know who got what. You and Mrs. Whipple, not to mention the museum, made out quite well. Harriman's brother did, too."

"Yes, but I know the family will contest, and I really don't expect to see any of the money." She looked pointedly at Dan, "So don't you go expecting any shiny, big presents from me, brother!"

He laughed. "I wasn't. Don't worry. All I need is the occasional six-pack to cure my woes."

Dulcie smiled quickly, then frowned, concentrating again. "So, it's the cousins, Jim Harriman, Alicia, Mrs.

Whipple, the museum, and me. We all have motives, in a way."

"Did anyone know about the will?"

"I certainly didn't. I don't think Alicia did. She was spitting mad."

"What about a basic motive of robbery?"

"I've thought about that. The Homer is so high profile that no one could have sold it openly. They'd have been caught in a second. If anyone wanted to steal it they would need an insider's knowledge of the art world, not to mention the black market, to profit at all. Not many people fit that bill. Just me, Alicia, Tom, and a couple of others at the museum who both have alibis."

"Do Alicia and Tom have alibis?"

"Apparently. Alicia was having a fling in Boston and was with a guy all night on Friday and Saturday morning. He vouched for her. Some research trip."

"My opinion of her remains unchanged," said Dan.

"And, Tom was at home with his mother."

"All right. We're up to Monday now. Monday was the funeral. Anything strange there?"

"Not really. Some tears, of course. I remember Tom had his arm around a woman who was crying. It must have been his mom. He just asked me for another couple of days off because she's shaken by this whole thing. Apparently she's very nervous that he's working where a killer could be on the loose."

"As am I," added Dan. "Why would she go to the funeral, though?"

"Who knows? You know how some people are. They need to pay their respects for one reason or another. Maybe she felt as though she was indirectly in Mr. Harriman's debt because he funded the museum internship for Tom?"

Dan nodded and stood up, taking her empty mug from her. "Could be. At any rate, you need to get some sleep now. I'll be here all night, so don't worry about a thing. I also noticed when I got the tea that your friend the detective has posted a police guard at the door, so you're safe." He leaned over and kissed her forehead. "Sleep tight, Sis."

"I'll try. Thanks, Dan." She closed her eyes and heard him lie down on the other bed again.

CHAPTER 11

Detective Black's alarm rang at five o'clock. He quickly got up, showered, gulped down instant coffee and half a cold bagel, then met Johnson outside of Alicia Harriman's apartment. Another officer silently hurried over and handed Nick a copy of the newly written search warrant. At five minutes before six they rang the bell and knocked loudly on the door. At last Alicia answered, very bleary eyed and very angry, wearing a silver-gray negligee.

"I'm sorry to bother you so early, Ms. Harriman, but we have a search warrant. May we come in?" As Adam Johnson barked out the words, it was more of an order than a question.

Her eyes grew wide. "*What?*" she screeched.

A well-muscled man appeared in the doorway behind her wearing only a pair of crumpled boxer shorts. "What's going on, babe?" he said to Alicia.

Alicia shook with anger as she stood in the doorway.

Detective Black said, "We need to search the apartment for an item connected with the murder of Mr. Joshua Harriman. If you'll step aside please, we will conduct the matter with as little interruption as possible."

Alicia glared at him but stepped away from the door. The man with her did the same. Nick walked into the apartment and directly into the bedroom, hearing Alicia let out a small gasp behind him. He went straight to the bedside table where Dulcie had told him he might find the statue. It was still there. He pointed to it, and Johnson took several photos before putting on gloves and carefully placing it in a plastic bag.

Nick turned to Alicia. "Can you tell me where this statue came from?" he asked.

She fumbled for words. "It was, um, a gift. From my uncle."

"When did he give it to you?"

"Um, last year. On my birthday."

"Can you explain, then, why it was seen two weeks ago in your uncle's study?"

"Who told you that? It was that bitch, Dulcie! She got all the money! She did it! She's just trying to set me up!" The man behind Alicia put his arm around her shoulders to reassure her, but she shook him off angrily.

"I don't think so," said Detective Black quietly. "Can you tell me the last time that you visited your uncle in his study?"

Alicia glared at him. Nick knew that look. He had seen it before. He waited silently. Slowly he saw the anger fade from her eyes and the first few hints of fear creep in, until terror filled her pupils. "I, um, I don't, um…"

"I'll help you. Was it last week?"

"Yes."

"Was it Saturday morning?"

She began to cry. "No, it wasn't! It was Friday night! He'd just come back from New York. I needed to talk to him. I needed money, but he wouldn't give me any! I was so angry, I took the statue without him knowing about it. I knew that I could sell it. I slipped it into my handbag. But, I didn't kill him! I swear, I didn't!"

Nick turned to Johnson. "Call for backup," he said quietly. "Turn the place inside out for the painting." He turned back to Alicia and took a deep breath, "Alicia Harriman, I am placing you ender arrest for the murder of Joshua Harriman. I must warn you that anything you say or do…," he continued with the standard speech. She cried hysterically. The man with her was hurriedly getting dressed.

"I don't know her very well! Really!" he kept repeating, hopping on one foot to pull on his trousers.

Nick looked over at him. "I'll need to ask you a few questions too, but I think that you may go afterward."

The police cruisers arrived. After waiting for her to get dressed, Nick escorted Alicia and her gentleman friend to the police station, leaving Johnson and the rest of the crew to find the painting.

ౣ

Three hours later, Nick returned to Alicia Harriman's apartment. Johnson met him at the door. "Nothing, yet," he said simply.

Nick rolled his eyes and leaned against the doorframe. "This is really getting frustrating. I had the lab run a quick check on the statue, and they can't find any traces of blood. Fingerprints of Harriman's, Alicia's, and the housekeeper's, but nothing else. They need to do more tests, but it doesn't look promising."

"So she couldn't have wiped it?"

"No, not unless she knows how to transfer the prints back on again. She's a smart lady, but I don't think she knows how to do that convincingly."

"No, not her area of expertise, I'd say," said Johnson, eyeing some lacy underclothes scattered on the floor. "Does it match the wound, though?"

"Unfortunately, yes. It has a rim around the bottom that matches the straight line gouge on Harriman's head." Nick shook his head and groaned. "We just don't have the right pieces here. I must be missing something."

Johnson looked over his shoulder at the police putting Alicia Harriman's apartment back in some semblance of order. "They've got it under control here, Nick. Want to get a cup of coffee?"

"Yes! Yes I do!" Nick looked at his partner gratefully.

They walked to a nearby cafe. Nick sat down wearily and looked at his watch. Johnson brought over two large cups of coffee, and they sat in silence for a few moments. Nick pulled a paper napkin from the dispenser on the table and clicked his pen.

"All right. Here we go. Again. Motive, means, opportunity." He wrote the three words across the top of the napkin. "Here are the possibilities." He wrote the names A. Harriman, J. Harriman, J. Whipple, T. Cole, D. Chambers, and Dan Chambers along the side.

Johnson looked at him very intently. "But, I thought we just arrested someone?"

"We did. Do I think she actually murdered him? No, I do not." He then added a final item to the column of names: a simple question mark.

"What's that for?" asked Johnson.

"There still could be a person that we haven't considered, or that we don't even know about, who killed Harriman. Someone in the right place at the right time."

"Pretty unlikely."

"Yeah, but we can't rule it out. Yet."

Nick considered the list. He began placing marks beside the names. A. Harriman: checks for motive, means, and opportunity. J. Harriman: checks for all three. J. Whipple: question mark for motive, check for means, *alibi* under opportunity. T. Cole: question mark for motive, check for means, *alibi* under opportunity. Dulcie Chambers: check for motive, check for means, check for opportunity. Her brother: question mark for motive, check for means, question mark for opportunity. He threw down the pen in disgust.

"God, I hate this job sometimes."

Johnson grinned. "With all due respect, no you don't."

"Yeah. You're right. And this," he gestured toward the napkin, "has to do with that damned painting. I swear to you, whoever has the painting killed Harriman." He looked up at Johnson from beneath a very wrinkled brow. "You know what we have to do next. We have to search the homes and offices of all our primary suspects."

"I'll start the paperwork," said Johnson. "Finish your coffee. You look like you need it. See you at the station?"

"Yeah. Thanks. I'll be there in a few minutes."

Detective Black slowly drank his coffee and surveyed the paper napkin in front of him. The names began to lose focus and swam around before his eyes. Motive. Motive. That had to be the key. "For some reason, I get the feeling that money is only secondary," he said to no one. He crumpled the napkin and stuffed it into his empty paper cup before tossing it in the trash on the way out.

Before returning to the station he stopped by the hospital. Dulcie was getting ready to go home. "How do you feel?" he asked.

"Fine. Still a little shaken, but physically fine. Just really tired."

"I'll stay with her today," said Dan. "Don't want any more mishaps."

"Good idea," said Nick. He turned to Dulcie. "Have you remembered anything else?"

"Well actually, yes. I was going to call you when I got home. I remembered that when I first approached Mr. Harriman's house on Saturday morning, I heard the housekeeper arguing with someone on the phone. I think it was her husband. Something about 'the gambling' and 'the racetrack.' I think he's been losing and she isn't happy."

"Are you sure she was talking with her husband?"

"Yes, as sure as I can be. I heard her call him 'Whipple' which she's said before when she refers to him. I don't even know his first name."

"Motive," thought Nick. "Is there anything else?" he said aloud to her.

"Well, not so much a memory as a conjecture. Last night Dan and I mentally walked through the events of the past few days. I remembered that when Mr. Harriman called me on Friday, he called the main museum number, not my cell phone as he usually does. I was the first to answer the call because I didn't think anyone was at the front desk to take it. Anyone in the museum at the time could have picked up an extension, listened to every word, and just kept quiet the whole time."

Nick's mind began to spin into action. "Who was there then?"

"I don't know. Tom and Alicia were both out. I think a volunteer was scheduled for the front desk, but you've said that they all have alibis. You'll have to check with security to know for sure who was there."

Nick nodded. "Anything else?" he asked as he rapidly took notes.

"No, that's all I can think of for now."

"This is good. Thank you. Take care of yourself," he said to her. Then he nodded to Dan and left.

Dulcie watched him leave. "Whew! His gears were turning!" she said. She gathered the few items she had with her, and Dan drove her home.

When they arrived at Dulcie's house, they were greeted by a police officer. "I'm sorry ma'am, but we have a warrant to search the premises."

Dulcie looked surprised, but unlocked the door and let him in. Dan tried to stop him by asking, "What's this all about? Can't you see my sister has…"

"No, Dan. It's all right." Dulcie interrupted. "I should have expected this, and probably you should, too. Neither of us has anything to hide."

"Me, too? They'll search my place? Why?"

"Because you are my brother and they know that we're close, which also makes you a possible suspect, or at the very least an accomplice. Think about it."

"I am, and I don't like it."

"I don't either, but there it is. You'd better go home and make sure they don't break anything."

"All right. As long as you have so many cops around, I guess you're safe no matter what they're doing. Will you call me when they leave?"

"Of course. Dan, thank you for looking out for me, but I am a grown-up, you know."

"I know, but ever since Dad died…"

"It's all right. Go home. I'll call you soon." She gave him a quick hug and he left.

Dulcie walked slowly back in to her living room.

"Could you unlock this for me ma'am?" The policeman pointed to a heavy set of flat files that stood in the corner.

"Oh, it isn't locked. The lock is broken. It just sticks. Tug hard."

The policeman did so, and the drawer came shooting out. He landed squarely on his bottom in the middle of the floor. His colleagues all laughed. Undaunted, he began sifting through the contents of the file. Dulcie had not opened it in nearly a year and was surprised at what the policeman found. He replaced the drawer and started going through the next one. Dulcie stopped him and asked if she could see the first drawer again. He pulled it out for her, more gently this time, and put it on the coffee table.

Dulcie sat down on her couch and began looking through. She found several old photographs from Mr. Harriman's childhood. She had forgotten all about them. He had given them to her and asked if she could have them framed for him. Dulcie felt terrible, knowing that she could never complete the task now, and worse still, that she had forgotten the simple favor that she had promised.

She looked thoughtfully through the photos, all browning with age. He had been a happy child, apparently. He was quite young in the first few. Dulcie found a date and his name scrawled on the back of one. The next few showed an older child with all the signs of becoming a handsome young man. She flipped to the last photo and gasped.

"You all right, ma'am?" The startled police officer was beside her in an instant.

"Yes," she said. She felt herself beginning to shake and was annoyed. She'd been doing far too much of that lately. "Yes, I'm fine. Do you know where Detective Black is right now?"

"Probably back at the station. Would you like me to call him for you?"

"Yes, I would. Thank you."

She went to her desk, pulled out a manila envelope and put the photo in it. Then she sat on the couch clutching it until the detective arrived. When he did, she handed it to him and said only, "An old photo of Joshua Harriman." He opened the envelope and looked at the photo. "I knew it had to be something like this," he said quietly. "Where did this come from?"

"In that flat file," Dulcie pointed. "He gave me some old photos months ago to be framed. I forgot about them completely."

Nick studied the photo again. "This is it," he said quietly. Looking back at Dulcie he whispered, "Keep this under your hat!"

Dulcie nodded. Nick departed quickly, leaving her in the midst of chaos in her own home.

CHAPTER 12

Alicia Harriman sat in the conference room at the offices of Hastings & Wexler with a snarl on her lips for the second time in a week. She had been released from her jail cell only that morning and obviously had little time to see to her usual beauty routine. Her hair was pulled back severely. Her makeup was harsh and heavy. She wore a tight, black, sleeveless turtleneck. She surveyed the others in the room with contempt, as though each was responsible for her recent experience.

The others at the table included Dulcie, Dan, Tom Cole, Tom's mother, Jane Whipple, her husband Jed Whipple, James Harriman, Mary Hastings, and Detective Black. Adam Johnson sat in a sturdy chair by the door leading into the room. Dulcie knew that two other police officers were in the hallway outside.

Mary Hastings stood. "I've called all of you here at the request of Detective Black. He thought that neutral ground would be best for the discussion that you are about to have. Since I am not a part of that discussion, however," she glanced at the detective who nodded in reply, "I will leave you to your business." She pushed back her chair and left the room.

Everyone at the table looked surprised.

Detective Black cleared his throat.

"As you all know, a murder has been committed. My colleagues and I have been working for the past few days to determine who is responsible."

"HA!" exclaimed Alicia under her breath. "We all know who that is!" She looked pointedly at Dulcie.

"We have called all of you here because you all have been suspects."

"Me?" said Mr. and Mrs. Whipple simultaneously.

"Yes. All of you either benefitted a great deal from Mr. Harriman's will, or at least thought you would. That would be sufficient motivation to speed up Joshua Harriman's death."

"Except Tommy and me," interjected Mrs. Cole.

Nick looked squarely at her. "No, Mrs. Cole. Every person here had a good reason for killing Mr. Harriman," he said softly. She blinked several times, and then looked down at the table.

"Let's go back through the past few days. A very expensive painting is up for auction. Joshua Harriman buys it in New York. He calls Dr. Chambers to tell her that he has it, and to say that he will contact her from his home the next morning. He returns to Maine with the painting late on Friday night. On Saturday morning,

Dr. Chambers hears nothing from him, so she goes to his house at noon, only to find him lying dead on the floor from a severe head wound. The police are called, and the investigation begins." A tap at the door interrupted Nick. Johnson rose from his chair and stepped outside for a moment. As he came back in, he leaned down and whispered in Nick's ear. Nick nodded.

"Let me continue," Nick said. "The investigation begins. The case immediately focuses on money. Mr. Harriman is an extremely wealthy man. However, unbeknownst to his family, he leaves the vast part of his estate to the Maine Museum of Art, a cool million to Dr. Chambers, a tidy sum to his housekeeper and his brother, and comparatively little to anyone else."

"Seems obvious to me," spat Alicia, glaring again at Dulcie.

"The money, however, is only one issue. Two other concerns were brought to my attention. First, the work of art that Joshua Harriman had just bought was missing. Second, there was a valuable statue missing as well from Harriman's study. We located the statue in the home of Ms. Alicia Harriman." All eyes turned to Alicia. She looked down. Nick remained silent, waiting through the long pause.

"He gave it to me," she finally muttered, squirming slightly in her chair.

"Did he? Your story seems to be constantly shifting, Ms. Harriman," said Nick.

"All right! He didn't! I came back from Boston late on Friday. I needed to pay off a debt, so I went to Uncle Joshua. He wouldn't give me a cent! He just laughed and said I had to learn how to earn my own way. He got up to pour a scotch and I saw the statue. I could have hit him with it, I was so angry, but I didn't. I just slipped it in my bag before he turned around. I knew I could get a few thousand or so for it, knowing the right people. Then I just left."

"And how much did you think you could get for the Homer?" asked Nick.

"I didn't take the stupid painting! Do you think I could have slipped that into my bag?"

Nick didn't answer her. He simply continued. "So, who else saw Mr. Harriman? I know that Mrs. Whipple arrives for her housekeeping duties on Saturday mornings."

"What! Do y'think I did it? I don't know nuthin' 'bout art!" she exclaimed.

"Yes, but you may have known that you were to inherit. Plus, you know enough about art to realize that Mr. Harriman's collections are worth a great deal of money."

"We're doin' fine, Whipple and me. What do we need with old Harriman's stuff?"

"Perhaps to cover those gambling debts?"

Mrs. Whipple froze.

Mr. Whipple turned white. "Those ain't much really, just... uh," Jed Whipple floundered wildly for words.

"Shut up, Whipple!" his wife said. "I ain't sayin' no more till I see a lawyah! If you're accusin' me, then go ahead!"

"I am accusing no one yet, Mrs. Whipple," said Detective Black. He turned to Dulcie. "This leads us to the next event. The person who discovered the body."

"Right!" said Alicia. Her eyes blazed.

Nick ignored her. "On Saturday morning Dr. Chambers hears nothing from Mr. Harriman, so she goes to his home at noon and discovers him dead. She cooperates with the police immediately. Does she have means to kill him? Yes. She could have come over earlier and hit him with any blunt object. Does she have motive? Again, yes. She stands to inherit a small fortune. Does she have opportunity? Certainly. No one was with her or spoke to her from Friday night until Mrs. Whipple saw her on Saturday at noon."

Dulcie sat calmly looking at Detective Black.

"Did Dr. Chamber's kill Mr. Harriman? No. I knew this when an attempt on her life was made, from which she very nearly escaped." He paused for a moment, hearing several gasps around the table. "I would like you to shift your focus to the painting that Mr. Harriman bought. This painting is very valuable. It also came with a bonus – an exact copy that could only be determined as such by the eye of an expert. Yet, that copy turned up in Dr. Chamber's coat closet at her office. Why would someone run the risk of taking both, and then plant the copy back at the museum? A clever forger could have created a convincing provenance for the copy, and both it and the original could have been quickly sold on the black market. It wasn't by any means one of Homer's greatest or better known works. No, the killer was not motivated by money. Money came into play only as a secondary motive."

"Then what did the killer want, if it wasn't the painting or the money?" asked James Harriman, looking tired and confused.

"Justice. But not the kind we think about ordinarily that takes place in courtrooms. The person who killed Joshua Harriman wanted to undo a wrong that had been committed more than twenty years before. Harriman was killed early on Saturday morning in a fit of rage."

"But, what about the painting? The Homer? Did the killer take that and plant the fake in Dulcie's office? How'd the killer know which was the fake, anyway?" asked Dan.

"By the way they were wrapped," said Dulcie turning to him. "The original was in a wooden box and was very carefully wrapped. The copy was in cardboard."

"That's right," said Nick. "Only after taking what looked like one painting, but then finding the second, did the thief realize the value of what he or she had. The copy was placed in Dr. Chambers' office closet to throw us off the track and point the blame in her direction. However, she soon learned of the copy from the auction house and knew that anyone with the right connections would keep the original and try to sell it. She believed that it was the copy that she found in her office. An expert proved her right."

"So where's the original?" asked Mrs. Whipple.

"Perhaps Ms. Harriman could tell us?" said Detective Black. All eyes turned toward Alicia.

"I don't... I haven't... *I didn't kill anybody!*" Alicia shrieked.

"No, I don't think you did," said Nick quietly. "Although you saw him dead, didn't you, and that frightened you. You returned to your uncle's house on Saturday morning, very early. You knew he had the painting and, knowing the security system in his house, you thought you could creep in, take it, and creep out again. It was a huge temptation, wasn't it? When you arrived though, you not only found the door unlocked, but your uncle was dead. You took the paintings anyway, then devised a plan that would divert suspicion elsewhere."

"That's ridiculous! Why would I do anything so stupid as to imply that Dulcie was guilty of stealing them? That would never stick."

Nick nodded. 'Of course it wouldn't, but it would throw us off track for long enough so that you could get rid of the original. You were able to do that quickly, but the statue was more difficult to sell. Not as many buyers for pre-Columbian works as there are for Homers, eh?"

Alicia sneered and looked away. Nick nodded to an officer standing in the corner of the room. He moved behind Alicia's chair and remained there.

"So now we turn to new motives: anger and justice." The detective picked up a manila envelope from the table in front of him. He pulled out the picture that Dulcie had found and flashed it quickly in front of the seated group, then put it face down on the table. "Do any of you know who that was?"

"Of course," said Mrs. Whipple. "It's Tom."

Nick looked at Dulcie. "No. It isn't," she said quietly.

"No, it is not," repeated Nick. "Mrs. Cole, could you tell us who this is?"

He held the photograph up again in front of Tom's mother. Her face had turned very pale. Usually quite pretty, even for her age, her face was now sunken and hollow. She whispered something.

"What was that, Mrs. Cole?"

Tom's mother swallowed hard. "It's Joshua Harriman."

The entire table gasped.

She looked up at them all, her eyes glittering with tears. "I knew him back then. He was so handsome, so friendly. He and I, well, we… but then he went away, and then little Tom was born. My husband, he didn't need to know. He's not so bright, and didn't even suspect. So, I just kept quiet. When Tom started working at the museum, well, I started thinking about it all again. I thought he had a right to know. I just never… Tommy!" Tears streamed down her face as she looked at her son.

Tom put his arms around her. She covered her face with her hands and sobbed. "It's all right, Mom," he kept saying to her, rocking her gently back and forth.

"She told me on Friday night, after I got home," Tom continued, still holding his mother. "I was so angry. Harriman had stood by and known for years while Mom struggled, trying to make ends meet. He didn't know at first, but when she told him, he did nothing to help her. Right after I got the internship Mom wrote to him and told him that I should know the truth. He told Mom that she should let sleeping dogs lie. He said that he wasn't going to tell me, and he wasn't going to help either me or her, other than to give me the internship. He said that it was enough to get me started in a good career. It was up to me to make my way, just as he had done. You know, he could have offered me all of his money, and I wouldn't have wanted a penny. Mom had worked so hard and suffered all those years. Nothing could make up for that.

"I went to have it out with him on Saturday morning. It was still a little dark. I knew he went to his study early in the mornings – we had talked so many times when I had taken him out to his boat in the launch. I had my big flashlight with me when I walked up to the house so that I could see. I turned it off and waited, then I saw him inside. He opened the French door in the study, then he left the room for a minute. I slipped in. I was just going to scare him when he came in, and tell him what I thought of him. But, when he finally did come in, and I saw him, I couldn't stand it. We argued and I just, I just…."

His mother sobbed harder.

"I couldn't believe what had happened. I knew he was dead as soon as he fell. I just ran. The flashlight was still in my hand. I ran down the street, back to my car and drove to Cliff Rock. Then I threw the flashlight as hard as I could into the ocean."

Now he was crying, too. He turned to Dulcie. "I'm sorry! I'm so sorry!"

The police officers descended upon him and took him away. His mother followed, her face wet and her eyes red and swollen.

No one at the table could look at anyone else. No one spoke for several moments until Dan said, "So the painting had nothing to do with the murder?"

Detective Black nodded. "That's right. We thought that we had only one criminal to identify, when in actuality, we had two unrelated events."

"You were going to let me rot in jail for killing someone when I didn't!" snapped Alicia.

Dulcie looked at her wearily. "I'm sure you would have had fine representation. You'd have served no more than ten to twenty."

"Shut up!" Alicia snapped.

Dulcie smiled at her. "By the way, I've just discontinued the internship program until further notice. You're fired." She had the satisfaction of watching two police officers handcuff Alicia, read her her rights, then escort her from the room.

⅓

Dulcie walked slowly back to her house with Detective Black. "So, what will happen to Tom?" she asked quietly.

"That's a good question. The murder of Mr. Harriman was a crime of passion. Hopefully a jury will understand that."

"What about the attempt on me? Do you really think he wanted to kill me?"

Nick suddenly stopped walking and gazed at her with astonishment. "I thought you knew!" he said.

"Knew what?" asked Dulcie.

He smacked his forehead with the palm of his hand. "Of course not! We've all been working so quickly, I didn't have a chance to explain it to you. Tom didn't try to kill you. Alicia did!"

"Alicia?"

"Yes. She thought that you were on to her scheme and, at the very least, she wanted to scare you away."

"Her scheme? You do mean the Homer, the copy, and the statue, right?"

"Not exactly. Have you been reading the reports of art objects being stolen from various smaller museums?"

"Yes, of course!" Dulcie gasped. "Do you mean to tell me…?"

"Alicia was the thief. Fortunately the 'buyer' of the Homer was an undercover FBI agent who had been investigating the thefts for some time. Alicia was eager to get rid of the Homer and was not as careful as she usually had been regarding potential buyers. With our help, the agent was able to nail her."

"You're kidding! Alicia? Do you mean that when I sent her on those various research trips, she was really stealing works of art?"

"Yes, unfortunately. She did a little 'freelancing' on the side, shall we say?"

"Unbelievable!" Dulcie was shaking her head. "Well, she'll get what she deserves now! What about Tom, though?"

Nick sighed. "I don't think that he wanted to kill anyone, really. He's lived a hard life and worse yet, watched his mother live an even harder one. To find out that it could have been much easier is a difficult fact to handle. He handled it poorly. I can't condone murder, but I do hope they'll be somewhat lenient on him."

"I agree," said Dulcie, "even though I hate the thought of what he did to Mr. Harriman. It's odd, though. I knew what had happened the minute I saw that photograph. I'm not sure how I knew, but I did."

"Yes. So did I. It's just one of those intuitive leaps that some people can make." He stopped walking again, and she stopped also.

"Dulcie? Remember that dinner?"

"You mean the one that I owe you?"

"Well, since you located the final clue, I figure we're probably about even. Actually, I think I really owe you now. What I mean to say is, would you like to go have it? Dinner, I mean? Right now?"

Dulcie sighed. "That depends," she said very seriously.

His eyes widened. "On what?"

"Well," she said, "are you off duty?"

A DULCIE CHAMBERS MUSEUM MYSTERY

FROM
THE
MURKY
DEEP

KERRY J CHARLES

FROM THE MURKY DEEP

CHAPTER ONE

He liked to run with his mouth open and his tongue hanging out on the left side. The kid took him to the beach quite often, and he especially liked to run there. It was early today, still a little misty. He took off as fast as he could go, down the beach, tongue hanging as always, ears flapping.

"Hey, Jack! Waitup!" the kid yelled.

'*Nope!*' he thought.

When he got to Big Rock sticking up out of the sand, he stopped. Jack loved Big Rock. So many great smells. If he was lucky, maybe something crunchy to chew on. He sniffed and sniffed, drooling a little on the slimy seaweed. He heard the kid walking up behind him, humming and dragging a stick in the sand. The kid liked Big Rock too.

Jack nosed around the edge of the hard stone and into the water lapping up against it. No waves today, really. Not much. He sniffed again and sneezed, sending chilly seawater spraying out in front of him. He shook his head vigorously making his tags clatter. Jack liked that sound.

He nosed into the seaweed a bit more. Now that smell was interesting! Kind of like a person and rubbery at the same time. He stopped and snuffled into it.

The kid came around the edge of the rock behind him, still humming. Jack heard him stumble, stop, and then make a strange noise. It was loud, like a yell and a scream all mixed up. Then he heard feet thumping against the sand. *'Oh good! We're going to run!'* Jack thought. He turned and launched himself up the beach trying hard to catch up with the kid, who was still making that odd sound.

CB

Detective Nicholas Black stood in the water looking down at the body. The photographer had just moved away. Nick had taken off his shoes and socks, and rolled up his jeans, but they were wet anyway. The mist had not yet burned off. It swirled around him, the rock, and the body lying in the water.

Nick heard heavy footsteps and a grunting sound behind him. "Stop being such a wimp, Johnson. Take your shoes off and get over here," he said, not even turning around.

"Yeah, well that's where you're wrong," muttered Adam Johnson and held up a pair of rubber boots, knowing full well that Nick didn't see them. Johnson groaned as he heaved himself down onto the sand. He took off his shoes and, rolling up his pant legs as best he could, shoved his feet into the boots. It took him several seconds to push himself up to a standing position again. "There we go," he said to no one in particular. He looked down and smiled at his work.

Johnson splashed into the water, managing to spray it onto the entire backside of his partner's jeans. Nick turned around with an annoyed look. "Do you mind?" he said.

Nick looked back at the body, encased in a full wetsuit and wedged against the large rock that jutted out of the sand. "What do you make of her?" he asked. First impressions counted. First impressions were the most important, and typically what people tended to forget.

"Quite fit," said Johnson. He leaned over and looked more closely. Without thinking, he stepped backward and began to kneel down. His bottom dipped into the ocean and one boot filled entirely with seawater. He jumped up, cursing.

Nick laughed. "That's the fastest I've seen you move in a long time!" he said.

"Damn cold water!" grunted Johnson. He leaned over without bending his knees this time. "Look at her scuba gear. Not new. Not rented either, I don't think. No markings like that. Either hers or borrowed from someone." He pulled out a pair of latex gloves from his pocket and snapped them on his hands. Gently he flipped her air gauge over to see the front. He looked up at Nick. "Empty tank. She ran out of air."

Nick kneaded the back of his neck. He'd been craning it at an uncomfortable angle to see everything he could without moving the body. "If it's her equipment, then she knows what she's doing. Strange that she would run out of air."

"Yeah. Agreed. Ready to move her?" Johnson asked. Nick glanced up at the beach and signaled to the photographer. She nodded.

"Yup. Emily's got all her pictures for now. Let's get a couple of these guys down here to help." He called to the uniformed police who had been skimming rocks on the glassy water. One of them let out a cheer as he counted eight skips. "Oooh, big winnah!" he heard another say. They all laughed and came over to where Nick and Adam Johnson were standing.

"Okay. Go time. Take off your shoes if you don't want to get 'em wet. Let's put her up on the sand," Nick said.

"Can we take the scuba gear off, sir?" one of the officers asked.

Nick looked at Johnson. "Guess we'll have to," Johnson said. "Just the vest with the tank and the weight belt. Leave the mask and flippers on if you can."

One of the officers moved forward and unbuckled the weight belt. He had trouble trying to get it off.

"Yeah, that's too heavy for Larry," another policeman said. They all laughed.

Nick had seen this before. Death was unnerving. Death like this was especially difficult. Humor was the only way that many could deal with it. He let the laughter die down then cleared his throat. "Let's get the vest and tank off all in one go. Unfasten it in the front, pull out the arm closest to the rock, then roll her into the water more. Peel the vest off as she rolls over." They managed without too much difficulty.

Her body floated easily in the shallow water, buoyed by the wetsuit. She was face up now. Nick looked at her again before they put her on the stretcher to carry her up the beach. Calm. That was the word that jumped into his mind. '*She looks calm*,' he thought. How could anyone be calm when they run out of air?

The police slid the stretcher under her easily in the water and carried her up onto the beach. They lowered the stretcher to the sand. "Let's at least take off her mask and gloves to get a look," Nick said. The mask came off easily, and left only red indentations on her forehead and cheeks.

Johnson pulled off her gloves. "No sign of grabbing or scraping really," he said, looking at them closely.

"Check her fingers," said Nick, still looking at the marks on her face.

"Nothing that shows any kind of struggle," his partner replied. "Look at this, though. Interesting. Looks like a phone number."

Nick swiveled around to look at the hand that Johnson held up. His mind began to whir furiously. '*No*,' he thought, but he knew that number. Whose was it? How could he know it? He shoved his hand into his pocket and pulled out his cell phone. Quickly, he scrolled through his contacts. Then he froze. "Oh my god," he said.

"What? What is it?" asked Johnson dropping the woman's hand. It landed on the sand with a soft thud.

Nicholas Black held up his cell phone to show Johnson the number that he had just found.

"Well, I'll be," Johnson murmured.

⚃

Dr. Dulcinea Chambers, "Dulcie" to those who knew her for at least five minutes, sat in a meeting with what she thought could be possibly the two dullest people in the world. They were droning on about file organizational systems for the museum's collections. Dulcie listened politely. As the director of the Maine Museum of Art it was her job to organize, oversee, follow through, make decisions…. She felt her cell phone ringing in her pocket. She'd turned it to "silent" mode so that it would only vibrate when a call came through. *'Damn,'* she thought. *'If only I could take it. It'd be the perfect excuse to get out of this meeting.'*

Dulcie looked at the two people across the table from her. When the one currently speaking stopped to take a breath, Dulcie quickly interjected, "You sound as though you have this well in order. Is there anything that you need from me at this point?" They both shook their heads. "Well then, let's go ahead with what you're proposing. It seems like a great solution and will make file searching lots faster." They both smiled and their heads bobbed happily up and down in agreement. "Keep me posted on the progress?" she added. Again, they nodded, and Dulcie stood. "Thanks for filling me in," she said and left. They had already begun talking again, ignoring her as she walked into the hallway.

Dulcie closed the door behind her with a sigh of relief. She reached into her pocket and pulled out her cell phone. "Huh!" she said out loud. "That's strange!" It read, "MISSED CALL: NICHOLAS BLACK." She checked her voicemail. No messages. Maybe he had dialed her by accident? She hadn't even remembered that he was still in her contact list.

Nicholas Black had entered her life several months before when the Maine Museum of Art's board chairman and chief benefactor, Joshua Harriman, had been found dead in his home. Nick and Dulcie had pieced together some unfortunate facts that had led to the arrest of the culprit. Although Dulcie and Detective Black had shared a very pleasant dinner together after the case was closed, she had not heard from him since.

Dulcie decided to call him, curious to see why he had contacted her or at least why he would still have her phone number. She quickly pressed the Call Back button on her phone.

Nick answered before the first ring had ended. "Dulcie," he said. "I mean, Ms. Chambers. Dr. Chambers."

She laughed. "Just 'Dulcie' is fine. Did you call me? I have your number listed but no message."

There was a moment of silence. "Um, yes I did." He paused, not sure what to say. He couldn't exactly blurt out that Dulcie's phone number was scrawled on the hand of a dead woman that he had just pulled out of the Atlantic. "I need to talk with you about something, but it's a little strange. Would you mind meeting me, as soon as possible?"

"Yes, of course," she replied. "You have me intrigued. I'm done for the day with my scheduled meetings, thankfully. You have no idea what a welcome relief talking with you would be."

"Don't be so sure about that," Nick said. He tried to make the comment sound lighthearted, but failed.

Dulcie was instantly concerned. "Do you have time now?" she asked. "Would you like to come to the museum, or meet somewhere else?"

"Somewhere else," he said quickly. "Can you be at Roaster's coffee shop on Commercial Street in about half an hour?"

"Yes, I can," she said nervously. "Does this have to do with the Joshua Harriman case?" She desperately hoped not. Dulcie had found it very difficult to reconcile her feelings toward his death. She hoped nothing would rekindle her anger and sadness.

"No, not at all. I'll see you in half an hour," he replied.

Dulcie checked the time on her phone then put it back in her pocket. She continued through the maze of hallways that surrounded the museum's public spaces until she reached her office. Leaving the door open, she sat at her desk and scanned through the schedule for the next day. Her assistant, Rachel, poked her head in. "How'd the meeting go?"

Dulcie rolled her eyes. "They have everything totally under control, as you can imagine. Our records are in good hands and will be absolutely thorough and complete. Beyond thorough and complete. Did I mention thorough and complete?"

Rachel giggled. Her curly brown hair bounced over her shoulders. "Better them than me!" she said.

Dulcie laughed and said, "Or me either! Rachel, I'm heading out for a meeting in a few minutes. I probably won't be done before we close so I'll see you tomorrow."

"Sounds good. Have a good evening!" she replied.

"You too," said Dulcie. With a quick wave, Rachel disappeared around the corner. Dulcie closed her laptop, slid it into her bag and slipped into her standard black blazer.

'Hmmm,' she thought. '*Nicholas Black. Now why didn't he ever really ask me out? I was sure he would after we had dinner that once. Maybe he thought I was too upset then.*' She paused after putting on her blazer, looking down at her petite frame in the outfit of the day. She was wearing a beige sheath dress with a black border at the hem and black leather pumps. *I suppose I could attempt to look a little less boring. Color in my wardrobe wouldn't kill me.* However, the thought of actually shopping put her off the idea once again. Dulcie detested shopping. Nothing ever seemed to fit quite right, and the lights in the dressing rooms always made her look like a corpse.

She shrugged her shoulders in resignation and picked up her tote bag. From their brief conversation it did not sound like her meeting with Nicholas Black would be much of a social call anyway.

When she stepped outside, Dulcie immediately took off her jacket. It was only a lightweight linen, but the August sun had been blazing down all day and the morning's wind was gone. She slowed her pace and thought, *'They'd better have iced coffee at the ready today.'* Everyone on the street seemed to be mimicking her, walking slowly in the heat.

She finally reached Roaster's and pushed open the heavy glass door. It took a moment for her eyes to adjust to the dim light inside.

Nicholas Black looked up as she came in, watching her blink several times. His heart lurched once, briefly. *'Get a hold of yourself,'* he thought. *'Don't be stupid. This is an investigation.'*

Dulcie spotted him in a booth, halfway through a cup of coffee. She quickly walked over and slid in opposite him. "Good to see you again," she said, smiling.

"You too, Dulcie. Really. I wish it could be under better circumstances."

Her brow wrinkled. "What do you mean?"

"Well, to put it bluntly," he glanced at his half empty cup, then said, "Oh, sorry!" interrupting himself. "Let me get you something." She started to protest that she could get her own but he was on his feet quickly. "No, let me get it. It's the least I can do after luring you here for something like this. What would you like?"

She smiled. Something about Nick always made her feel at ease. His voice was quiet and strong at the same time. "Iced coffee. Milk and sugar please," she said.

"Good. Be right back."

Dulcie watched Nick give her order and chat with the woman at the counter for a moment. '*He must come here often*,' she thought. Then she remembered that the police station was only a block or so away. *Bet this coffee is way better than what they have there.* She smiled, imagining those terrible coffee vending machines that squirted out various syrups into hot water.

Nick came back, sliding her iced coffee and a straw along the table to her, and replacing his own cup with a fresh one.

Dulcie took a long sip. "Perfect. Thanks! Now, you were saying…."

"Yes. It isn't pleasant." He took a deep breath. "A body washed on shore this morning. A scuba diver. Looks like she ran out of air."

"Good god, that's awful!" said Dulcie. "But, how can I help? I've done some diving, and I'm certified, but you must have people to do that for you."

Nick looked surprised. He hadn't expected her to be a diver. "No, we don't need any help from that angle at this point, but there is something else. We can't identify her yet, but we do have a lead. Kind of an unusual one." He had been spinning his cup around on the table somewhat nervously. He made himself hold the cup still and looked her squarely in the eye. "Dulcie, it seems that your cell phone number was written on her hand."

Dulcie squinted at him. "My number?"

"Yes," said Nick, "and I'm afraid, if you don't mind, I need to take your cell phone to check all incoming and outgoing calls." He looked slightly embarrassed.

Dulcie sat back in the booth and scrutinized him for a moment. Then she took a deep breath and shook her head slightly as if to clear away confusion. "Of course," she said and pulled the phone out of her pocket. "How long will you have it?"

"We'll try to finish with it quickly. I'm sorry. Do you have any idea who this woman could be?" Nick asked.

"No, but I might have a better idea if I knew what she looked like, perhaps."

Nick pulled out his own cell phone. He looked up at her. "Can you handle this? Pictures of a dead person?"

Dulcie swallowed hard. "Yes, I think so, if they aren't too graphic."

"No, mostly she looks like she's asleep." He handed the phone to her with a picture of a woman's face on the screen. Dulcie studied it. "Are there more?" she asked without looking up.

"Yes, you can scroll through."

Dulcie flicked through the images. Something looked familiar about the woman. She was probably about Dulcie's age. Had she been in the museum recently? Perhaps.

Dulcie took a long pull on the straw and gulped her coffee. Then she looked up at Nick. "She looks familiar. I can't place her, but I'm pretty sure that I've seen her before. Maybe at the museum?"

"That might explain the phone number. Do many people know your cell number?"

"It isn't public, but it certainly has been circulated enough. Quite a few people have it at this point."

"All right. Well, if you could just keep thinking and let me know if you remember anything else about her. I'll get your phone back to you as quickly as I can, hopefully by tomorrow morning."

"Thanks, I appreciate that. It's my lifeline, unfortunately." She looked at Nick curiously. "Is there anything else? It seems like I don't have quite the whole story."

He'd forgotten how quick and intuitive she was, and for a moment it caught him off guard. "Nothing that I can tell you right now," he said.

"Well then," she replied. She took one last sip of cold coffee and slid out of the booth. "I'll wait for you to get in touch? You can call me at the museum." He nodded. "Nick, there's nothing else you can tell me? It could help me remember something."

"I'm sorry, but I really can't say anything else right now. We're in the early stages."

"I understand. I'll just do my best," Dulcie replied. "I'll talk with you soon." She picked up her jacket and bag, and quickly left.

Nicholas Black had stood as she was leaving. He had been bred to stand when a lady entered or left the room, and it was now a mechanical instinct. He slowly sat again and took a deep breath, looking down at her cell phone. He had not told her the most critical piece of information. Along with the body of the woman, they had found a watertight tube. Rolled up in the tube was what appeared to be an incredibly valuable van Gogh painting which, he had just learned, had been stolen from a private collection the year before.

Dulcie was at the top of the suspect list.

Nick didn't like it.

If you would like to read more of the Dulcie Chambers Museum Mysteries please visit the author's website (kerryjcharles.com) for more information or request copies at your local bookstore or library. Ebook versions are also available from major suppliers online.

Reviews from thoughtful readers are always welcome on any website or media outlet. Thank you!

ABOUT THE AUTHOR

Kerry J Charles has worked as a researcher, writer, and editor for *National Geographic Magazine*, the Smithsonian Institution, Harvard University and several major textbook publishers. She holds four degrees including a Master's in Geospatial Engineering and a Master's in Art History from Harvard University. She has carried out research in many of the world's art museums as a freelance writer and scholar.

A swimmer, scuba diver, golfer, and boating enthusiast, Charles enjoys seeing the world from above and below sea level as well as from the tee box. Her life experiences inspire her writing and she is constantly seeking out new travels and adventures. She returned to her roots in coastal Maine while writing the Dulcie Chambers Museum Mysteries.